"The cream of British mysteries."
Publishers Weekly

"Top-drawer...Blowing the lid off a cozy English village is a noble pastime, of which Sherwood is an able practitioner."

New York Daily News

"Sherwood knows his territory and understands human emotions while the horticultural lore is enticing even to one who can barely recognize the difference between petunias and geraniums."

Murder ad lib

"Celia Grant will delight and entertain mystery enthusiasts. Celia is every bit as clever and endearing as Agatha Christie's Jane Marple....A wonderful book to curl up with on a chilly winter evening."

Chattanooga News-Free Press

"Delightful and unexpectedly poignant...Delicious tidbits for gardening enthusiasts, much wry English irony, and an acerbic send-up of contemporary English village culture, with its nouveau snobs, its insular garden fete contingent, and its close-ranks old-timers. Miss Marple would have loved to have had Celia Grant's insights."

The Kirkus Reviews

Also by John Sherwood
Published by Ballantine Books:

MENACING GROVES
FLOWERS OF EVIL
THE MANTRAP GARDEN
A BOTANIST AT BAY
GREEN TRIGGER FINGERS

A BOUQUET
OF
THORNS

John Sherwood

BALLANTINE BOOKS • NEW YORK

Copyright © 1989 by John Sherwood

All rights reserved under International and Pan-American Copyright Conventions. Published in the United States of America by Ballantine Books, a division of Random House, Inc., New York.

Library of Congress Catalog Card Number: 89-6265

ISBN 0-345-36525-9

This edition published by arrangement with Charles Scribner's Sons, an imprint of Macmillian Publishing Company.

Manufactured in the United States of America

First Ballantine Books Edition: May 1991

❧ ONE ❧

"When did the accident happen?" asked Celia Grant.

"An hour ago. She was on her way here."

"Can't we juggle with the times a bit? If she'd done her stuff and had the crash on the way back, there'd be no problem."

Ann Hammond thrust a pencil into her untidy bun of grey hair and scratched with it. "Wouldn't there? I don't get it, this is too deep for me."

"I could nip in quietly and do the job and everyone would think it was her."

Ann treated her to a bull-like stare. "You must be bonkers, Celia. Half the village would see you nipping in and out. Besides, if she was going home her car would be pointing the other way. If we told fibs the constabulary would be on us like a flash."

An officious traffic cop lived in the village, Celia remembered. "Horrors, yes. I'm sorry, Ann. If I can't be anonymous I daren't risk it."

Frustration made Ann Hammond's precarious hair-do collapse in ruins. "You must, damn it. There's no one else."

She stood up, large, imperious and untidy, the picture of a ruthless female bully. Celia, by contrast, was small and fragile-looking. Though her hair had gone prematurely

1

white, her figure was neat and youthful and she had the complexion of a china shepherdess. But she was a lot tougher than she looked, and not at all easy to bully.

"There's no one else." Ann Hammond repeated, "and very little time,"

This was true. The entries in the Melbury flower show were already laid out in the village hall, waiting for the judge to inspect them and award the prizes. The elderly lady who had judged the show for the past twenty years was in Welstead General Hospital being patched up after her car accident. Some stand-in had to judge the show before it opened to the public in less than two hours' time. As the owner of a flourishing horticultural business Celia was the obvious choice, but she was determined not to be the fall guy. The rules and regulations governing village flower shows bewildered her. Entries of cottage pinks and runner beans were judged under conventions as strict and abstruse as those applying to severe Japanese gardens made of stones and sand. Dark and earthy passions could rumble on for weeks if an exhibitor thought her flower arrangement or her husband's plateful of beetroot had not been given its due by the judge. Celia attended this curious annual event conscientiously. Though she was happy to consider herself debarred as a professional from competing, she usually sent in one or two rarities from her stock to be exhibited out of competition.

"You'll have to do it, Celia," Ann argued. "Everyone else who knows enough has entries in half a dozen classes."

"Can't we leave it unjudged as a mark of respect and sympathy?" she suggested.

Ann Hammond hooted with laughter. "She gets no respect or sympathy from me. She's eighty and blind as a bat and she's driven her car into a ditch and cracked a rib or two, serve her right. You'll have to do it, Celia. Who's qualified to if you aren't?"

Unfortunately she had a point. Celia had a good degree from a horticultural college, and had shared plant-hunting expeditions in three continents with her husband, who had been a leading light at the Royal Botanical Gardens at Kew. After his early death she had started a small business specialising in rare plants, more or less as a hobby, and had been astonished when Archerscroft Nurseries turned out to be a roaring commercial success. But these were not the right qualifications for judging Melbury's annual flower show.

"Ann, I don't know enough," she protested. "I'd hate all the things I ought to drool over and give prizes to all the wrong people. I'd be hung, drawn and quartered in front of the village hall."

"No you won't, because I'll be there. I'll tell you what prizes to give to who."

"Then why can't you step into this dangerous breach and do the judging yourself?"

"I shall, but you'll have to take the rap because I've got entries in seven classes, it would look bad. Do come along, we're wasting time, you know you'll have to say yes in the end."

Celia hesitated. She longed to refuse, but one had to be very tough to say no to bull-like Ann Hammond with the loud voice and the collapsing hair. She was the wife of the local doctor, who had practised in Melbury for almost forty years, and she had the whole intricate range of village politics at her energetic fingertips. She was the secretary of the Melbury Parish Council and a churchwarden, and was actively involved in almost every other village activity including the annual flower show, of which she was the secretary.

"Oh, very well," said Celia. "But give me five minutes to fix things here."

It was a Saturday, and the frame yard of Archerscroft Nurseries was full of customers. Both the Saturday girls had turned up for work, so they and the regular staff could cope with the flow at the sales counter without her. She caught her head gardener, Bill Wilkins, between two sales to customers, and told him what she had been bullied into doing.

"Oh no, Celia. Don't you dare, that flower show's a snake pit. You put one foot wrong, and they'll have your toenails off of you."

"Mrs. Hammond's going to be at my elbow and protect my toenails with her advice."

Bill grunted something cross but indistinct and went back to his work. Celia returned to the office block, where Ann Hammond was waiting impatiently. They drove in convoy down the lane into the High Street, and parked behind the village hall, a pleasant building presented to the village by a Victorian squire. George Tunney, the chairman of the flower show, was waiting for them in the porch. He was a handsome greyhead in his sixties, and had been the foreman at the now defunct paper mill which had once been Melbury's main employer. Nowadays his energies were divided between occupying key posts in village organisations and producing unnecessary quantities of oversize vegetables in his garden.

"Thank goodness ye're here, Mrs. Grant, we were in a right sweat with the old girl not showing up. We all know her likes and dislikes, and we've chosen what we show according. Ye'll be judgin' along the same lines as her, I hope?"

"I'll try, with some prompting by Mrs. Hammond."

"That's right," Ann shouted genially. "And you'll keep her on the straight and narrow over the veg, George. Better get down to it now, we've not much time."

A riot of colour and scent greeted them inside the hall. "Class one," Tunney read out. "An arrangement of flowers in tones of any one colour, foliage of a different colour permitted."

"First prize to Mrs. Carpenter," Ann decreed. "The one with the dahlias."

Celia was surprised. The cards with the exhibitors' names on them were all turned face down, so that personalities could not influence the judge. "How d'you know whose it is?" she asked.

"Dolly Carpenter's been using that vase for years."

4

Celia disliked the combination of flame-coloured dahlias with hectic yellow and green foliage from an *Elaeagnus pungens*. But she turned the card up obediently, and Tunney attached a first prize sticker to it.

"How about this one for second prize?" she suggested. It was a pleasantly informal composition in silver and shades of pink.

"No!" cried Ann.

"Why? What's wrong with it?"

"Look at that huge rose, right at the top of the arrangement. That's no way to win a prize, you have to put the big flowers at the bottom and the small ones at the top."

"Goodness, why?"

"They call it 'making a centre of interest'. This is hopeless, one of the yuppie women from the executive housing estates must have done it. Nice of them to bother, but they don't know the form."

With the new fast train service the village was within easy commuting distance of London, and four bedroom two bathroom houses had been built on the fringes to cope with the executive influx. Some of the incoming wives had been shrewd enough to see that a flower show entry might be a passport to acceptance in the village, but not shrewd enough to master the labyrinthine rules.

They worked their way through five more classes of flower arrangements. The conventions of "floral art" were very strict. If wire or other supporting material was used in the vase, not a glimpse of it must be visible, even from the back. Everything had to be in perfect condition, a pin-size insect hole in a leaf was enough to disqualify. The ideal arrangement, it seemed, was pyramid-shaped, with the flowers at the bottom shooting out downwards from the vase, the sort of florist's arrangement which conveys the message: this is a very expensive restaurant.

Most of the pyramids had been confected by hardened ladies from the gentrified period houses and cottages in the picturesque High Street. Celia obediently awarded one first prize, two seconds and a third to Ann Hammond, "Because

I usually win a lot," she guffawed. "If I draw a blank people will think it odd." Ann's other decisions were even more arbitrary. One woman edged her way into first place because she had just come out of hospital, and a rather mediocre entry for "an arrangement in a wineglass," received a prize to cheer her up because "her dreadful spotty daughter's run away to live with her boy friend in a squat in Brixton."

"What on earth's this?" asked Celia as they dealt with class ten. "A basket of flowers arranged for effect."

Among the splendid wicker baskets cascading blossoms in all directions there stood a dismal little straw affair containing a few wilting wildflowers and even, if one was being uncharitable, weeds.

"It'll be from them funny people with the goat," said George Tunney.

"Of course, Mrs. pain-in-the-neck Tidmarsh," Ann agreed. "Typical, she would."

The neck that the Tidmarshes were a pain in was Celia's. They were Londoners who had bought the smallholding next to Archerscroft Nurseries, and taken to country ways with more enthusiasm than expertise. Their earthy lifestyle involved a loving relationship with seed-scattering weeds, grey squirrels, moles and other nuisances which did not respect property boundaries, including a goat with wanderlust and a voracious appetite.

"How silly of her," said Celia. "She only entered that squalid mess so that she could despise us for not seeing how superior it is to everything else."

Pot plants came next. "This ought to get first prize," Celia decided, pointing to a bushy plant with succulent jade green leaves, beautifully grown and displayed in a famille rose pot. A small label identified it as *Aichryson bollei*.

"Give a prize to that?" Ann objected. "The damn thing's not even in flower."

"It wouldn't be, it flowers in September. They come from the Canary Islands and they're so rare that they're almost extinct. I've never seen a better grown specimen."

"I daresay, Celia, but the village won't know that. What d'you think, George?"

"We could do with something a bit showier," Tunney decided. "How about that streptocarpus?"

The streptocarpus had an unusual colour break, pink with a blue throat, Celia recognised it. She'd given it months ago to Joan Berridge, who worked at Archerscroft, on her birthday, but also as a thank you for turning up at work with a frightful cold in March, when the rest of the staff was off ill. She was a very stupid woman, but a green-fingered genius with pot plants.

"She deserves first prize for putting up with that shocker of a husband," said Ann.

"He's my nephew," Tunney reminded her sharply.

"I daresay, but he's still a shocker," Ann retorted.

There was no love lost between them, Celia remembered. They were both prima donnas with pretensions to leadership in the village. She let them put the streptocarpus in first place, but argued that the *Aichryson* deserved a prize too. "Can't we make it second?"

"Who on earth sent it in, let's see." Ann flipped over the card to look at the competitor's name. "Mrs. Bradshaw. The new people at the mill. We ought to encourage the newcomers to send in entries, so very well if you insist. Okay by you, George? Second prize for this boring little bush."

Celia made a mental note that Mrs. Bradshaw was interested in rarities and might be worth cultivating.

The next few classes were for growing flowers rather than arranging them. Six stems of sweet peas. Rambler roses, four sprays, any variety. Ditto climbing roses. Six stems or sprays of border pinks, any variety. Three delphinium spikes. Here, the workaday population of the village came into its own, and George Tunney took over from Ann as judge of the finer points. Briefed by him, Celia picked her way through a minefield of sensibilities and regulations, and decided among other things that the butcher's enormous sweet peas were marginally superior to the postman's, that

7

the right order in the carnations class was first prize Andrew Berridge of the garage, second prize Charley Englefield of the village shop, and third prize George's wife Kathleen because, according to him, she "went grouchy" unless she won something and her entry was "no worse nor anyone else's."

The vegetable classes, the most numerous in the show, were also dominated by the workaday village. Their council houses in Summerfield Close, built by the local authority in the 'fifties, had gardens large enough for each family to be self-sufficient in vegetables and provide plenty over for the show. Guided by Tunney, Celia learnt that for show purposes peas could be uneatably large and hard provided they filled the pod to bursting, that what counted with onions and gooseberries was their enormity, and that runner beans which were not as straight as rulers had to be straightened artificially before they were shown. The old lady had operated a rota system, making the leading vegetable exhibitors take turns with the first prizes from year to year, and George could not remember whose turn it was to win the "collections," each containing potatoes, onions, carrots, runner beans and peas. "Is it me or Arthur Berridge? Darned if I can remember. Give it to Arthur, I don't mind."

The next hurdle for Celia was home produce. "Must I really taste twenty-four pots of home-made marmalade?" she asked.

"Hell, no," said Ann. "You just look through the glass. Make sure the bits of peel are all the same size and evenly distributed, that's the form, and the round of greaseproof paper on top has to be exactly in the middle, that's very important. You cut the cakes in half. Choose one where the currants haven't all floated to the bottom, and give it the prize."

The public would have to be let in almost at once, and the children's drawings remained to be judged. "No, not that one," Ann Hammond advised hastily. "The girl's much too conceited already . . . Yes, that's clever, but the mother's very pushy, I bet she helped the child draw it. How about this? The father's just lost his job, it'll give the family a lift."

As she fixed on the prize stickers, George Tunney opened the doors of the parish hall, and the public began to come in.

The flower show was one of the highlights of Melbury's summer, and every section of village society was there. Cheerful families from the council houses in Summerfield Close whose elders, two generations ago, had vacated the picturesque but inconvenient hovels in the High Street in favour of the subsidised comforts of public housing; professional people who had gentrified the High Street hovels into comfortable homes; a few couples from the new executive houses, who stood about shyly trying to make their entrée into Melbury society. It looked like a peaceful mix of people enjoying themselves, but it always looked like that on the surface. The reality was different. Everyone resented the executive houses and kept their occupants at arm's length. The shopkeepers and Summerfield Close resented the way Ann and her friends talked patronisingly about "the village," by which they meant those inhabitants of Melbury who did not qualify as gentry. A powerful faction in the gentrified High Street thought that Ann Hammond was altogether too bossy in her handling of Melbury's affairs, and the whole of Summerfield Close backed George Tunney, as the leading figure among the council house dwellers, in his resistance to her bossiness. "The village" kept itself to itself, and guarded its secrets from outsiders. But behind its curtain of reserve it was a welter of tensions, jealousies and shameful secrets that everyone knew but nobody ever mentioned. As Celia stood with the bustle and noise of this seemingly happy gathering swirling round her, she did not foresee—how could she?—that she would soon find herself dragging one of those secrets out into the light with most of the village against her, and that by the time she had finished two people would be dead.

"Good afternoon, madam," said a quiet voice at her elbow. It belonged to Burchett, the manservant of Colonel

Templewood, the biggest landowner in the parish. Burchett had dyed black hair, a papery white skin, thin bloodless lips and an insatiable curiosity. He had been the colonel's batman in their army days, and the village considered him a sinister figure.

"These roses are very nice," he murmured. "I wonder why they were unplaced?"

Celia looked at the exhibit, a collection of twelve specimen rose blooms, and tried to remember why she had been made to reject it.

"You did judge the show, madam, didn't you?" said Burchett. "Someone had to be found to do it quick, in the circumstances."

The old lady's accident was not widely known yet, but it was typical of him to know about it. He collected information as a dung-beetle collects dung, and was frequently believed to carry back what he collected, some of it not very savoury, to his employer.

Celia had managed to find the small earwig bite in an outer petal of a Grandpa Dickson which her advisers had detected, and pointed it out to him. He went away satisfied, having trapped her into telling him what he wanted to know, namely that she had judged the show.

Moving around the exhibits, she found herself face to face with her tiresome neighbour Wendy Tidmarsh, who wore a dirty off-the-shoulder sweater and cotton skirt, and had an equally dirty little girl in tow. "So our little basketful of wildflowers didn't find favour," she remarked with a superior smile.

"I think it belongs in a different kind of show. Why don't you start an alternative gardening society for people who go in for that sort of thing?"

"Would you join it? No, I suppose not, you use poisons."

Celia used pesticides very sparingly, but was not prepared to say so. "I'd have less reason to use chemicals if you didn't let a mass of thistledown fill our seedbeds with dandelions."

"But dandelions are so pretty, much prettier than the rare

plants you grow to sell to garden snobs. And they make such delicious salad.''

"Dandelion salad's yucky, I hate it," said the little girl.

"It's very nice if you get the dandelions young," Celia told her. "The salad wouldn't be nasty and bitter if your mummy picked them before they flowered instead of after.''

Changing the subject hastily, Wendy Tidmarsh embarked on a diatribe against the use of pesticides. "It's perfectly easy to control pests by biological methods. I'll send you a leaflet if you like.''

"Thank you, but I use *Encarsia* and *Phytoseiulus* in the greenhouses."

"I daresay, but why use poisonous chemicals when you can get useful insects to attack the bad ones and control the pests that way?''

"*Encarsia*," said Celia with creamy venom, "is a wasp which lays its eggs in whitefly at the scale stage of their development, and kills them. *Phytoseiulus* is a predatory mite which attacks red spiders. It's a very efficient control system, and I don't think I'd learn much from your leaflet.''

Turning away smartly from this demolition job, she was accosted by George Tunney's son Ron. He was a traffic cop, who supervised the nearby motorway in a gaudily painted police car, and spent his spare time setting an example of solemn rectitude to the village. He dragged her over to the pot plants to inspect Joan Berridge's prize streptocarpus.

"Joan says you gave it to her, Mrs. Grant. Is that right?''

"Yes."

"On her birthday?''

"That's right. Why?''

"Her birthday's March twenty-third, I know 'cos she's my cousin. Well then.''

"Well then what, Ron?''

He produced the schedule of the show, and read from the rules. "A pot plant 'must have been in the possession of the exhibitor for at least three months prior to the show.' Joan's hasn't, it's over a week short. It's disqualified.''

Voices were raised in Joan's defence. It was only a matter of a few days, why bother? George Tunney, as chairman of the show, had to arbitrate. He was soon surrounded by a tight huddle of people arguing in undertones, for "the village" preferred to settle this sort of delicate problem quietly in private. Fat Joan Berridge, the cause of all the fuss, stood on the fringes of the group with a sleepy expression on her bespectacled moon face. How typical of her, Celia thought, to make a muddle over dates. The woman was a genius with plants, but an utter fool over everything else. It was doubtful whether she had really grasped what was going on.

The matter could have been settled quietly if Simon Berridge, Joan's "shocker" of a husband, had not arrived to join in. The Berridges and the Tunneys were two huge families which intermarried constantly, and formed a tightly organised clan within the village. This did not prevent individual Berridges and Tunneys from pursuing quarrels with each other whose origins were lost in the mists of time, and one of these was between Simon Berridge and Ron Tunney. Simon's mother was George Tunney's sister, which made him and Ron first cousins. Ron was a solid citizen with a steady job in the police force and no sense of humour. Simon was a beer-swilling ne'er-do-well, a work-shy casual labourer with a permanent two-day growth of beard and a glass eye which made him look even more disreputable. His sense of humour was overdeveloped and Ron was one of his favourite targets.

He had arrived drunk from his long midday session at the Red Lion, and rushed at once to the defence of his wife.

"Ye silly gormless police prick," he shouted, rounding on Ron. "It's only a tiny mistake, there's no need to make a long face like a mixy rabbit."

If Ron disliked being compared to a rabbit with myxomatosis, he showed no sign of it. "A rule's a rule," he droned. "Ain't that right, Dad? Once you let people bend the rules, where are you?"

"Pharisee!" Simon yelled, glaring at Ron with his glass

eye while the good one went wildly astray. "Joan's only a few days out, why carry on as if she'd strangled someone's baby?"

"I think we should give her the benefit of the doubt," said George Tunney.

"Now now, what's all this about?" asked Ann Hammond, muscling into the group. When the problem had been explained to her, she said. "Of course we must stick to the rules. Sorry, Joan, but we can't bend them. That's right, isn't it, George?"

George Tunney glared at her. It was for him, not her, to interpret the rules. He began to protest angrily, but Ann's ruling had made Simon even angrier. He seized the controversial streptocarpus from the exhibition table and deposited it at Ann's feet, causing the pot to shatter and earth to spread in all directions. With a rude gesture, he pushed his way past her and lurched drunkenly out of the hall.

"Well, it's certainly not getting a prize after that," she decreed.

Joan Berridge had stood passively by during all this, and Celia suspected that she retreated into a mental cocoon whenever she was faced with unpleasant events, and pretended to herself that they were not happening. But the sufferings of a plant were a different matter. Within seconds she was on her knees uttering low moans of concern and scooping up the remains of the streptocarpus.

Later, when Celia was talking to a group of women who worked at the nursery, she caught sight of Bill Wilkins' handsome blond head looming above the crowd as he elbowed his way through it towards her. He had gone white and his nostrils were quivering, a sure sign that he had lost control of his low-flashpoint temper. Something must have gone very wrong at Archerscroft.

"That cheeky goat of the Tidmarshes was at the seedbeds again," he reported. "There's half a dozen of them special hellebores gone, and heck knows what besides. That's the third time this month."

The Tidmarshes' goat was a recurring problem. New to

13

country ways, they did not know how to tether it properly, and it had formed a habit of bursting through the hedge and over the rabbit-wire to browse on succulent patches of rarities being raised in the Archerscroft Nurseries' seedbeds.

"Mrs. Tidmarsh was here a moment ago," said Celia. "I'll speak to her."

"No, I will," said Bill, and darted away in search of her. Celia was alarmed. His fits of temper had got worse lately. If he was too rude to the Tidmarshes they would break off diplomatic relations with the goat problem unsolved.

He found Wendy Tidmarsh over by the soft fruit. Her husband was with her, a stringy undersized forty-year-old with granny glasses worn askew. After listening patiently to Bill's torrent of reproach, he said softly, "We are sorry if our goat has trespassed, and quite see why you are angry. We will try to ensure that it doesn't happen again."

"You said that last time it got in, and the time before," Bill raged.

"But Mr. Wilkins, what more can I say?"

"You can shut up about how everyone but you gardens all wrong, and you can learn how to tether a goat properly."

"Don't like goat's milk, it's yucky," piped the Tidmarshes' little girl.

"And you can stop letting your weeds seed themselves all over us," Bill concluded.

"We are sorry if our style of husbandry offends you," said Tidmarsh. "Unlike you, we believe in letting nature take its course whenever possible. I think it will be best if we refrain from mutual criticism and try to see each other's point of view."

"Well my point of view is, it's the owner's responsibility to keep his animals fenced and under control. And if that animal gets loose again and does damage, I'll shoot it."

Wendy Tidmarsh gave a gasp of horror. "Oh no! Shoot Gertrude? You couldn't be so heartless."

"I could and all."

"I would advise you strongly against doing that," said Tidmarsh.

"Why? I'd be within me rights."

"Violence breeds violence," said Tidmarsh, straightening his granny glasses and glaring through them. "I am a peaceable man, but I can be very violent when roused, so be careful what you do."

"Yes, yes, shoot Gertrude, goat's milk's yucky," insisted the little girl.

The afternoon was wearing on, and Celia wished they would get on with the prizegiving and have done with it. But a pair of newcomers had just entered the hall, a thickset man in his forties with an air of authority and a somewhat younger wife. Their arrival seemed to be causing a minor sensation, and Celia asked Ann Hammond who they were.

"The new manager of the paper mill and wife. Name of Bradshaw."

The picturesque old mill on the river, a once thriving business manufacturing various specialised lines of paper, had fallen on evil days and gone bankrupt. After standing empty for several years, it was about to start up again under a new owner. According to village gossip, a paper mill in London's East End had changed hands in a takeover deal by an asset-stripping conglomerate whose main interest was to sell its valuable site. Rather than close down a profitable subsidiary, it had bought the derelict mill cheap and was moving the machinery from London into it.

The Bradshaws had settled into the mill house several weeks ago, but this was their first public appearance in Melbury. They were inspected with interest, especially by Summerfield Close, which was getting its first look at a possible future employer. Celia paid more attention to Mrs. Bradshaw who was, she now realised, the owner of the *Aichryson bollei* which had interested her so much. She was a tall, dark woman, striking looking but not handsome, who had retained into her thirties the gawky movements of an awkward teenager, and Celia decided at once that she was still agonisingly shy. Her husband had gone to chat in a well-judged public relations exercise with a group of men who had worked at the mill before it closed, so she was standing by herself in the middle of the room, looking helpless. Celia went up to her and introduced herself.

"Oh. How d'you do? I'm Eileen Bradshaw."

Celia complimented her on the *Aichryson bollei*, which turned out to have been grown from seed, and explained about Archerscroft Nurseries.

"Oh, but I've got your wonderful catalogue," exclaimed Eileen Bradshaw. "As soon as we're properly settled in I'll be up there picking your brains and spending more than I can afford. The garden at the mill's in a terrible state, I'll have to start from scratch."

It soon became clear that she was a knowledgeable plantswoman, and her shyness vanished as she talked. Celia took to her instantly, but was distracted by what was going on around her, for the pair of them were surrounded by an interested circle of spectators. Eileen Bradshaw was the centre of all eyes. Burchett, Colonel Templewood's inquisitive manservant, was studying her with beady-eyed concentration, as if she presented him with some sort of riddle. Four Summerfield Close grandmothers were staring openly and muttering to each other, as if they were not sure whether or not they had recognised a television star. When Eileen Bradshaw's husband called her away they began arguing aloud.

"T'isn't."

"It is. It's her, I bet you."

"She was only a kid when she left. You can't be sure."

"It's the spitting image of her. And the same awkward way with her arms and legs."

"Would she come back, after what happened?"

"You'd have to if your husband was made manager of the mill."

"If it's her, why would she be pretendin' it isn't?"

"Wouldn't you? Think of the disgrace."

"I'd not come back, I'd be ashamed."

"But it is her. I swear it is."

Celia's besetting sin was curiosity. As soon as she could, she sought enlightenment from Ann Hammond. "There seems to be a lot of excitement about Mrs. Bradshaw."

"Oh, that. A lot of batty old women have been cackling like hens, silly creatures. All because there's a resemblance between Mrs. Bradshaw and a girl who left the village years ago under a cloud."

"Really? What sort of cloud?" Celia asked.

"Have to tell you later," Ann murmured, and moved to the door. Colonel Templewood, who was to give the prizes, had just arrived.

The Templewoods were landowners whose nine hundred acres of prime arable land protected the south side of Melbury from developers anxious to build yet more executive-style houses for commuters. Successive generations of Templewoods had been generous benefactors of the village, and the village hall had been a gift from the colonel's grandfather. Only a few years ago, the colonel himself had contributed almost the whole cost, which was considerable, of reroofing the church. He was a tall, distinguished-looking figure in his seventies, with an outstanding record for bravery, Celia had been told, in the Second World War. He was a widower, respected in the village but too aloof to be popular, though older people had affectionate memories of his dead wife.

As he looked briefly round the exhibits, Burchett sidled up to him and murmured something which he greeted with an alarmed look and a non-committal grunt. Then he made a stiff little speech praising the skill of the exhibitors, and began to distribute the prizes, small sums in cash in envelopes. As the winners came up to receive them they were greeted with a thin smile of congratulation from the colonel and a round of applause from the onlookers, whose enthusiasm varied with the popularity or otherwise of the recipient rather than the number of prizes he or she had won.

"Mrs. Bradshaw," George Tunney called as he handed the colonel the envelope. "First prize for pot plant."

Of course. With Joan Berridge's streptocarpus disqualified, the *Aichryson bollei* had moved up from second prize to first.

Mrs. Bradshaw walked clumsily up the room towards the colonel with her face set in a wooden expression which seemed to cover some strong emotion. The colonel's fixed smile of congratulation slipped for a moment, as if he too had been struck by the resemblance which the gossiping grandmothers had noticed. The grandmothers clapped so vigorously that Eileen's routine round of applause became an ovation. It was as if they were applauding the climax of some drama, Celia decided, in which Mrs. Bradshaw and the colonel were the leading actors and Burchett, watching intently from the sidelines, played an important supporting role. But what was the drama?

The prizegiving was soon over. While the men adjourned to the Red Lion for refreshment, the women washed up crockery in the kitchen at the end of the hall, for tea and biscuits at tenpence a time had been served throughout the festivities. As in duty bound Celia joined in. She and Ann Hammond were busily drying teacups when Mrs. Bradshaw appeared, carrying her pot plant. "Oh!" she exclaimed, and halted awkwardly in the kitchen doorway. Silence fell among the washers-up.

"Hello there. Does that thing need water?" Ann asked her.

"No. I was just taking it home. The car's round at the back."

Ann gave her a bull-like stare. "But you can't get out to the car park this way. You'll have to go out through the front."

Mrs. Bradshaw seemed much more embarrassed than her mistake warranted. She fidgeted in the doorway, tried to say something and thought better of it, then turned on her heel. The kitchenful of village women looked after her as if they had seen a ghost.

"There now, it is her after all," said one of them as they recovered from the shock. "Must be. It's Barbara Berridge."

"Who is Barbara Berridge, and what was that all about?" Celia asked as she and Ann Hammond left the hall.

"There used to be a way out to the car park at that end. Blocked up years ago, when they added the kitchen on. Barbara Berridge wouldn't know that, it was after she left the village."

"I see. So when Eileen Bradshaw tries to go out that way, the washing-up contingent decides that she must be Barbara Berridge in disguise, despite her pretensions to the contrary."

"Yes. She seems to be Barbara Bradshaw now, though."

"But if she's who they think she is, why does she call herself Eileen and deny all knowledge? Surely she can't have expected to get away with it?"

"It's a long time. Eighteen years. People's looks change. Barbara must be thirty-three now, she was fifteen when she left."

"Under a cloud?" Celia asked.

"That's right. She was going to produce an illegit."

"An illegit's not much of a cloud, even for a fifteen-year-old. Doesn't the village take that sort of thing in its stride?"

"Usually. This was a bit special."

"How, special?"

"Come in and I'll explain. I owe you a stiff noggin anyway, after all that judging."

They were walking along Melbury's High Street, a much photographed composition of picturesque houses and cottages ranging from the fifteenth to the nineteenth centuries. The Hammonds' was in a group of graceful Georgian village houses built by prosperous farmers and small gentry as winter quarters, in which to enjoy a neighbourly social round while knee-deep mud made the lanes between their outlying farms impassable.

Settled with a large whisky in one of Ann's chintzy armchairs, Celia said, "Now. Tell me all. Why was Barbara Berridge's pregnancy so special?"

"Simple. The younger Templewood boy was supposed to be the father."

"Oh really Ann, what's special about that? Landowners' sons have been betraying village maidens for centuries, to no one's surprise."

"Don't you know what happened? What Paul Templewood did? No, I suppose not, it was before your time."

"I think I've heard vague rumours, but remind me."

Eighteen years ago that October, Ann explained, it had been Colonel Templewood's turn to be host to the local shoot. His son Paul, then sixteen, was there. He had been tense and worried for some time. Suddenly he had run amok for no obvious reason and started shooting at the beaters. "He killed or wounded half a dozen of them, mostly lads that my Jack had brought into the world. Simon Berridge got pipped in the eye, that's why he has to have that glass affair that looks so awful."

"And what happened to young Templewood?" Celia asked.

"Paul? Turned the gun on himself in the end. Sensible, what else could he do?"

"Oh Ann, what a ghastly story."

"Yes, a shocker. Old Templewood never got over it. Never held a shoot since, or let anyone else shoot over his land. And look at what he's spent on the village over the years. Soon after it happened he paid to have that kitchen added on to the village hall. Lots of things after that, and then the church roof last year. Guilt money, all of it, because of what his son did to the village."

"Including the relatively minor matter of getting Barbara Berridge pregnant."

"Oh, but that wasn't minor, there was a nasty angle came out at the inquest. Paul had been frantic for money, borrowing and not paying it back, stealing too, bits of silver and so on that he could sell. No one could make out why. By then Barbara Berridge had started vomiting up her breakfast, and her unsuspecting family hauled her off to Jack's surgery where the obvious was pointed out and the family dragged out of her the news that Paul was responsible. So why hadn't she spoken up before? Answer, she'd been blackmailing him on account of the bun in her oven, and that made him so uptight and miserable that he lashed out with his shotgun.''

"In other words," said Celia, "Barbara was morally responsible for the massacre because she drove him crazy.''

"That's right, and she'd made it worse by keeping mum till it was dragged out of her. There were a few mutterings afterwards about how she was an easy lay and any of the village boys could have been the father, and she'd picked on Paul for the money. But that story got stamped on double quick by the Tunney-Berridge mafia.''

"In case it reached the Templewoods?" Celia suggested.

"I suppose so, but Jack always says something funny went on then, something he didn't understand.''

"And how did the Templewood family react?"

"They may have smelt a rat, I don't know. They'd have paid up anyway; after Paul's performance they were too racked with guilt to ask questions. Templewood came to Jack's surgery and fixed for Barbara to be packed off up north somewhere to have her baby. That was the last anyone heard of her, we all thought she'd gone to the bad.''

"Ann, you don't really believe that Eileen Bradshaw is Barbara Berridge in disguise?''

Ann hesitated for a long time. "Could be, there's a likeness if you allow for the age difference. Barbara had the same sort of bony face and clumsy movements, and the same way of cringing, as if she was apologising for not being better looking. She's shy, so was Barbara. What convinces me, though, is her thinking she could get out through the kitchen to the car park.''

"That's not conclusive," Celia argued. "It could have been a stranger's innocent mistake.''

"A stranger wouldn't have been embarrassed into a fit of the fidgets like that.''

"How about a shy stranger racked with guilt about not helping with the washing up? Besides, fancy going back to the village where you were brought up and pretending to be someone else. Would you, Ann?''

"No. But I'm not a batty ex-juvenile delinquent."

"Where did Barbara fit into the vast Berridge tribe?" Celia asked.

"Her father was a real tearaway, that boy was, wrote himself off driving an unlicensed car with no brakes. Drunk I imagine, he usually was. The wife died soon after that, viral pneumonia I think Jack said, but it was really being left with no money, no husband, not even a rotten alcoholic one, and two small children. She was George Tunney's sister, so when she died George and Kathleen took charge and brought Barbara and Simon up."

"You mean, that wreck with the glass eye is Barbara's brother?"

"That's right. Booze runs in the family. On the male side, anyway."

"But Ann, this is even more incredible. Fancy living in the same village as your own brother and keeping him at arm's length."

"At arm's length is the right place for Simon Berridge."

"But can you imagine going back to your home village and putting on this extravaganza?"

"You would if there was a cupboardful of skeletons you hadn't told your husband about."

"Oh. I see what you mean. Bradshaw doesn't even know that she was born and bred here."

"That's right. Put the squalid past behind you and say you're Eileen not Barbara."

"Surely you'd have to tell your husband?" Celia objected.

"Okay, let's suppose he knows the whole story, and they decided it would be less embarrassing all round if she pretended."

"No, Ann. Suppose you're the husband, and you've been told. Would you take your wife to live in a village where she had the reputation of being an easy lay? To be pointed at by a lot of married men in their thirties who had her when they were teenage louts?''

"Ah, but that's not what she'd tell him," Ann argued. "Only a lot of guff about her star-crossed love for the squire's son, who went mad with tragic consequences."

"If that's your story, you're a victim and a sympathetic figure. You are now a respectably married woman and your husband sees no reason why you shouldn't be reunited happily with your family despite the little slip-up all those years ago. There's no way the thing makes sense, and I am driven to the conclusion that Eileen Bradshaw cannot be Barbara Berridge."

So that's the end of that, Celia thought as she drove home. She was determined not to get involved, she was much too busy. Not that there was anything to get involved in. But it was an interesting little puzzle to play with.

❧ TWO ❧

"There was another of them scatty bunches left for me this afternoon," said Bill Wilkins as he and Celia stood in the frame yard discussing the work schedule for the next day.

"From an unknown admirer, no doubt," she said, for Bill was ridiculously handsome in a blond Viking manner, and the sight of him often made otherwise sensible women behave like lunatics.

"If it was that, you'd think they'd take more trouble," Bill grumbled.

What he called the "scatty bunches" were odd-looking little bouquets of miscellaneous flowers, put together with no regard for aesthetic effect. This was the third time it had happened.

"Where was it?" Celia asked.

"In me kitchen, on the draining board. It's always the same place."

"Can I have a look at it?"

"Come on in."

The gardener's cottage opened directly on to the frame yard. Bill was the well-organised type of bachelor, and his kitchen was aggressively neat and clean. He retrieved the miserable little bouquet from the waste bin under the sink and presented it for Celia's inspection. It was indeed a "scatty bunch," consisting of one moss rose bud, one sprig of heliotrope, one bright red ranunculus, one sprig of mallow and a piece of dittany, all bound together untidily with a rubber band.

"How odd," Celia commented. "It looks more like witchcraft than floral art. Who can be behind it?"

"Our naughty half-mad neighbours," he suggested, "putting a hex on me because I said I'd shoot their goat."

"The Tidmarshes are very eccentric," she admitted. "But I don't think it's them. They're wildflower fanatics, they'd rather die than have anything to do with a fussed-up hothouse thing like heliotrope. Besides, where would they get hold of a bit?" She picked up the flowers and frowned at them. "Are they the same ones as before?"

"Not quite. Last time there was a sweet pea and no heliotrope, and a bit of white clover. The time before I don't remember, except that there was a whacking great tulip, a red one, and a forget-me-not."

Celia had a sudden and alarming flash of insight. "Oh horrors, I think I know what this is about. D'you mind if I take these home with me and look one or two things up?"

"Home" was an exquisite little Georgian doll's-house, a hundred yards down the lane from the nursery. Living there embarrassed Celia a little, it was almost a parody of the appropriate dwelling for a tiny woman with hair that looked like an eighteenth-century powdered wig. One of the bedrooms had been fitted up with shelves, in which she had installed a fine library of botanical books that she and her husband had collected during his time at Kew. She found the book she wanted, opened it and confirmed that her hunch was correct. It was the mention of the forget-me-not that had done the trick—in this context it could have only one meaning.

Bill had always been strictly a one-girl man, reacting with puritanical disgust to the constant invitations to promiscuity which his good looks entitled him to. Since his steady girl friend's death two years ago he had given a very rough time to starry-eyed admirers who offered themselves as replacements, something that happened all the time. He would be furious when he realised that some half-baked female was making overtures to him through the Victorian language of flowers.

The book she had taken down from the shelf was *Le Langage des Fleurs*, by "Charlotte de la Tour" (a pseudonym), published in Paris in the eighteen-thirties. It was the first of a host of manuals on the subject, for the language of flowers had enjoyed enormous popularity among the repressed Victorians as a means of furtive communication between the sexes. Many of the books published in England merely translated the flower meanings given by de la Tour. But there was a rival school of thought which derived some of the meanings from Shakespeare, notably from the coded flower references in the Ophelia scenes of *Hamlet*, so that rosemary had to mean "remembrance" and not, as de la Tour would have it, "your presence revives me." Some authors thought French meanings such as "*volupté*" for tuberose were too indecent for the tastes of Queen Victoria's prim subjects, and changed them. All in all, the disagreements between the various guides to the art of floral communication were so wide that lovers attempting to reach an understanding but using different books must often have ended up in hopeless confusion.

But there was no doubt about the message of Bill's posy. A bud from a moss rose was a confession of love. Dittany meant "passion" and heliotrope meant "devotion." The ranunculus announced "I am dazzled by your charms" and the mallow that "I am consumed by love." The sweet pea and the red tulip in earlier posies had similar meanings. But what lovelorn female was responsible? Bill's kitchen door, which opened on to the frame yard, was seldom locked. It was marked "Private," so a customer slipping into it would be conspicuous, but an Archerscroft employee would not. The culprit was probably one of the giggling girls who dealt with mail orders in the packing shed.

As Celia expected, Bill was disgusted and angry when she announced her findings in the morning. "Oh Celia, that's kinky, that's nasty. Filthy little hot-pants, I'll learn her, you wait till I find out who it is."

Celia was determined to prevent this. If he discovered that it was one of the mail order girls, he would make her life such a misery that she would throw up her job in floods of tears. It had happened before, and mail order girls were hard to replace. At all costs he must not identify the culprit, and she had made arrangements to frustrate him.

"I've brought a few flowers with me," she told him, laying them out on his kitchen table.

"What's all this then, Celia?"

"The rue and the moss rose come from my garden at the cottage. I snitched the snapdragon and the tansy from the Taylors' front garden, and I tore my tights getting the gorse out of the hedge. Gorse means 'anger' and a snap-dragon means 'presumption'. Rue means 'disdain', tansy means 'I declare against you', and if you stick the moss rose in upside down it becomes a confession of hate rather than a confession of love. Unfortunately I couldn't find a mandrake which means 'horror', but I think the message will be clear enough to choke whoever it is off."

"You mean, you want me to put this lot on me draining board for the silly slut to find? If I do that I won't get to know which of them it is."

"Exactly, and I won't have to find a replacement for her when you've made her life a misery and she resigns."

Grumbling a little, he let her arrange the floral rebuke in a beer mug on his draining board. For three days it remained there, while he invented unnecessary jobs for himself in the frame yard so that he could spy on anyone entering his kitchen door. On the fourth day it vanished while he was busy pricking out double primrose offsets in one of the nursery beds. Next evening, when he came in from the day's work, he found that his unknown correspondent had delivered a reply.

"It's all weeds," he told Celia. "Come and tell me what it means."

"Dear me, that huge piece of gorse must mean 'I am

even angrier than you are,' and I don't like the look of that nettle. Come along to the cottage when you've changed and we'll look them all up.''

He came. As she poured him a drink she noted, not for the first time, how tatty his off-duty clothes had become. His open-necked shirt was frayed at the cuffs, and there were stains on his slacks. When Anthea was alive, he had been a discreetly trendy dresser. This was not the only thing about him that her death had changed for the worse.

"I've been looking up your bits and pieces," she told him, "and they're rather disturbing. The stinging nettle means 'cruelty', the buttercup means 'ingratitude' and the burdock means 'rudeness'. That's bad enough, but there's this centaurea, which I think must be the nearest she could get to a Scotch thistle, and also a very worrying bit of birdsfoot trefoil. The thistle means 'retaliation', and the trefoil means 'revenge'."

"Oh Celia, what nerve. How dare she?"

"I could kick myself for being so stupid, now we'll never know who she is."

"That was what you wanted, I thought."

"Yes, but I didn't expect this, I thought our rude message would choke her off, she'd just go away and have a good cry and that would be the end of it. What does she mean by revenge? Weedkiller in the seedbeds? Sabotage in the glasshouses? Horrors, it doesn't bear thinking of."

"We got a wrecker in number three glasshouse already. There's some sort of virus got at them little cyclamen."

"Oh? How bad is it?"

"There's a lot up at one end, the new leaves are all twisted and brown."

This was worrying. The house contained almost a thousand seedling corms of the tiny, heavily scented *Cyclamen libanoticum*, which was rare enough to bring in a hefty profit.

"I'll get Peter Verney to look in tomorrow and tell us what it is."

Bill made a face. "Him? Oh Celia, must you?"

Peter Verney lived a short way up the lane from Celia. He worked at an agricultural research institute on the other side of Welstead which specialised in biological pest control. She had relied on him heavily for advice on keeping her glasshouses free from whitefly and red spider without using chemical sprays.

Bill groaned. "Oh Celia, must we fiddle about getting insects to eat each other? I'll give them a good dose of Endrin tomorrow."

"How d'you know the thing on the cyclamen isn't a resistant strain?"

"I'm resistant to mucking around with the glasshouse temperatures all the time to keep your insects happy."

There was a long-standing disagreement between them over this. Celia did not believe in slinging pesticides around unnecessarily, and many glasshouse pests had developed resistances to them. Admittedly, biological control was a little more trouble, because pest and predator had to be kept in balance. If the tiny *Encarsia* wasp did not have enough whitefly to lay its eggs in, the next generation of wasps would not be there to deal with the next infestation of whitefly. Conversely, the whitefly could get the upper hand by laying too many eggs for the wasp to cope with. But the whitefly needed high temperatures for optimum egg production, and the wasp much lower ones, and for this reason the ventilation lights in the glasshouses were constantly being opened or shut, without regard for the convenience of the plants. Bill often complained that the glasshouses were being used for insect culture, with plants as a low-priority sideline.

"I'll get Peter to drop in tomorrow on his way home and have a look," Celia told him. "I'll be seeing him tonight."

Bill reacted sharply. "Where's Verney taking you out to?"

"Nowhere," she said coldly. "He's a parish councillor. There's a meeting tonight."

Celia had been elected to the Parish Council after taking part in a successful protest against a threat to the village from a hypermarket, and had been regretting it ever since. The meetings were a crashing bore, but she attended them out of a sense of civic duty.

"Why do you dislike Peter so much?" she asked.

"Oh Celia, he's not right for you."

"What on earth d'you mean?"

"Had you not cottoned on? He's divorced, he's on the loose. He's after you, the horny little sneak."

Celia was so astonished that she burst out laughing.

"Stop that, it's not funny," he shouted in a burst of bad temper.

"But Bill, he's at least ten years younger than me, I'm not a baby-snatcher and I'm sure the idea never entered his head."

"Oh it did, Celia. You wait and see."

"Nonsense—but now I'm going to turn you out, the meeting's at half past seven and I don't want to be late."

As she drove down to the parish hall, she worried about Bill. He had always had a hot temper, but now he had sour fits of the sulks as well. There had never been even the faintest overtone of sex in her relationship with him, but he had become insanely possessive. This was not the first time he had tried to break up a harmless friendship of hers with a man. Verney's advice to her tended to happen over a drink at his house or hers, that was all the thing amounted to. Because of her fragile appearance she tended to over-stimulate the protective urges of men. But she kept her eyes open for signs of overheating in her relationship with them, and usually managed to lower the temperature before any-one's feelings were hurt.

Though perfectly contented with her celibate lot, she was not above fantasising from time to time about a man she found interesting. When the Parish Council was called to order by its chairman George Tunney, she sat down opposite Peter Verney, and as it ploughed through its long agenda, she studied him. He was solidly built and might run to fat later, but she fancied chunky men rather than the slim and elegant type. His hair was dark and curly, and the overflow at the neck of his sports shirt hinted at more of it elsewhere. He interested her, but when she tried to imagine herself in bed with him, she recoiled from the idea.

She woke from her fantasy to discover that the meeting was discussing a right of way over a footpath through a field. It had lapsed years ago, having formed part of a network of paths used by Victorian farm labourers walking to and from work, and was of no value to ramblers. But a keen new member from the executive estate was proving his love for the countryside by trying to get it reopened. The law was on his side, but the path was on Colonel Templewood's land and no one wanted to offend him, least of all George Tunney. He floundered about in the chair without finding a way out until Ann Hammond, who was the parish clerk, intervened and rescued him by fudging the issue competently.

"Any other business?" Tunney asked.

"I've got something," said Ann. "Mr. Bradshaw has asked me to find out if the council would like to be shown round the mill now that most of the new machinery has been installed. He thought we'd like to know what the process involves and what workforce will be needed and so on."

Amid a rumble of approval the invitation was accepted and Ann was instructed to arrange a suitable date. The meeting broke up and Celia buttonholed Peter Verney about her problem with the glasshouse full of cyclamen corms.

"I doubt if it's a virus," he said. "It sounds more like cyclamen mite to me."

"I looked in on my way down here. There's nothing like a mite to be seen."

"There wouldn't be, they're too small. I'll call round on my way home tomorrow and we'll make sure."

He made a long face when Celia showed him the damage next evening. It was mainly concentrated at one end, but obviously serious. On many of the corms, the young leaves were distorted and roughened-looking. One or two were completely dwarfed and had tiny leaflets which had failed to open properly. There was no sign of pestilent insects.

Peter lifted up one of the pots and brought out a magnifying glass. "Ah yes. You can't see them properly without a high-powered microscope, but they're there, the damage is characteristic. You've got an attack of *Tarsonemus pallidus*."

"Which in ordinary English means what?" growled Bill.

"It's variously referred to as the cyclamen mite, the begonia mite and the strawberry mite. It attacks all three, and a lot of other ornamentals as well."

"So how do we get rid of it?" Celia asked.

Before Peter could answer, Bill said, "Give them a good drenching with Endrin."

Peter corrected him gently. "I'm afraid spraying with an insecticide wouldn't be much use. The sneaky little beast tends to lay its eggs in clusters in leaf and flower buds where a spray can't reach them. I'd try biological control if I were you."

Bill snorted and made a disgusted face.

"There's a fierce little predatory mite called *Ambliseius mackenzii*," Peter suggested. "It's much less fussy about its food than the predatory wasps, and it's been used to control cyclamen mite before. You could try that."

"Fine. Where do I get it?" asked Celia.

"There's a chap in Holland who rears it on a flour mite, I've got his address in the office."

"But getting it from Holland will take days," Celia protested, and Bill made a tetchy movement of impatience.

Peter thought for a moment. "I could probably get you some from the lab. Leave it with me and I'll see what I can do."

Noticing Bill's thunderous expression, Celia hurried Peter away before the outburst happened.

Next morning, Mrs. Bradshaw came and spent almost an hour looking round the nursery and making notes. "Oh dear, what a lot of lovely things," she exclaimed, with a comic look of despair on her bony face. "I've made a huge list, but that garden at the mill is a shambles, I can't plant anything till I've got it tamed."

"If you would like to give me an order for the autumn, I can reserve things for you," Celia told her.

"Oh, that would be kind. But it's a small garden, and I want far more than I've room for. You . . . wouldn't come and look and let me pick your brains about what to have?"

"I'd be pleased to."

They made a date, and in due course Celia drove down to the mill house, a gracious example of old-world weatherboarding with its front facing the pool which fed the millrace. It was reached from the working part of the mill by a footbridge over the mill-race with its long disused waterwheel. The garden overhung the river on the downstream side of the house, and would be charming when it was put in order. Mrs. Bradshaw welcomed her with almost pathetic eagerness, as if she needed friendship even more than advice about her garden. As they walked round it and discussed planting schemes, Celia decided that she liked Eileen Bradshaw. In a horticultural context her shyness vanished quickly and she became very relaxed.

"I'll see you tomorrow, then," said Celia when it was time to go. Eileen looked puzzled, so she explained. "I'm on the Parish Council. Your husband's invited us to see round the mill, and we're coming to you for drinks afterwards."

"Oh yes. Of course." Suddenly she was rigid with tension. Was it, Celia wondered, the reaction of a very shy person at the prospect of acting as hostess to a largish party? Perhaps. But if she was Barbara Berridge under an alias, there would be an extra reason for nervousness. George Tunney, the chairman of the Parish Council, was her uncle. The members included Mrs. Englefield from the village shop, who was born a Tunney, Chris Wood the postman who was married to a Berridge, and several more village people who must have known her as a teenager and witnessed her disgrace. Did she really expect to get away with it? What had she told her husband, and how had he received it? Whatever the answers, she was clearly someone who needed a friend.

Next day the Parish Council duly visited the refurbished mill, and was initiated into the mysteries of making multiply computer paper. Production could not begin until an essential piece of machinery had arrived and been installed. But as soon as it did, Bradshaw assured them, local labour would be recruited and trained to supplement the key workers who were transferring from the old site in London. When he had shown them the efforts being made to clear the weed from the millpool and tidy it up, they all trooped across the footbridge above the frothing water which flowed out of it over the weir and down the mill-race to the huge wheel, now still, which had powered the mill in the days before steam and electricity.

On the far side of the bridge lay the mill house and the Parish Council trooped into a charming drawing room where Mrs. Bradshaw was waiting beside a drinks table, deathly pale and under rigid self-control. Celia watched her closely. When George Tunney approached her, she offered him some cocktail snacks with an appalled dead-pan look. But perhaps it was just her shyness. She wore the same look when confronted with Ann Hammond, and with the new council member from the executive estate.

The afternoon's programme had been presided over not by Bradshaw, but by a superior of his from head office who had arrived at short notice on a visit of inspection. During the guided tour he had broken into Bradshaw's explanations with unhelpful remarks of his own which interrupted the flow, and he now showed symptoms of wanting to make a speech. Having reduced everyone to silence, he said how happy he was that his visit to the mill had coincided with theirs, since the firm's policy was to promote maximum co-operation with the communities in which it operated. Moreover, he wanted to tell them what a sterling fellow Ted Bradshaw was, and what a useful addition to the village he would be. Having done so in considerable detail, he held up his glass to Eileen. "And don't underrate his charming wife Barbara, who is not just a lovely girl and a delightful hostess, though she is both those things. But she also has a first class business brain. Before she married Ted she was Miss Berridge of our accounts department, and no unnecessary expense got past her."

Unaware that he had just dropped the verbal equivalent of a nuclear bomb, he held out his glass in her direction. For a moment she stood there, rigid with horror. Then she hid her face in her hands, brushed clumsily past her uncle and half a dozen other councillors who knew her history, and bolted out of the room.

Assuming that she had suddenly been taken ill, the distinguished visitor decided that he had charmed Melbury Parish Council for long enough. "Don't bother to show me to my car, Ted," he said graciously. "Go and look after her."

Bradshaw was very red in the face. He began to say something, but realised that nothing useful could be said and went after his wife. The distinguished visitor shook hands graciously with the Parish Council and went away in a haze of self-satisfaction.

"I hope Mrs. Bradshaw's illness isn't serious," said the new member from the executive estate.

No one bothered to explain to him. The Parish Council was blank with shock. Should they leave tactfully or stay? George Tunney, confronted with a niece who had refused to acknowledge the relationship, was deeply shaken, but managed to give a lead. "I reckon we'd best go."

"Yes, end of drinks party, don't you think?" Ann Hammond agreed. "They'll want to sort it out quietly together, so off we go, and I'll write a line to thank them."

The Tunney-Berridge mafia filed out to put their heads together and hammer out a common attitude to the problem they faced: how was the village to treat a returned juvenile delinquent whose husband seemed likely to become Melbury's main employer?

"Well, that was a bit of a shocker," said Celia as she and Ann walked to their cars.

"Damn silly of her," Ann commented as she fingered her collapsing hair-do. "There was no need to pretend, it's all past history now."

Was it really past history, Celia wondered? Or was this the start of the next instalment?

Next morning she was struggling over a muddle with invoices when Ted Bradshaw walked into her office. "I've come to explain about last night, d'you mind?"

Celia made him sit down and prepared to listen.

"Barbara likes you a lot, Mrs. Grant," he began. "She wants to have you as a friend, and she's afraid the thing yesterday will put you off."

"It won't, I like her," said Celia. "We've a lot in common."

"So she asked me to come and explain. I tried to make her come with me, but that business back in the 'seventies hurt her so much that she gets quite hysterical if she tries to talk about it. You know what happened?"

"In outline, yes. She had an illegitimate baby and was accused of blackmailing the father, who went crazy and shot a lot of people."

"That's right, and she was so ashamed that she left the village for good and blotted the whole thing right out of her mind. She'd even invented a different childhood for herself; about how her parents had been killed in a car crash, and she'd lived with foster-parents till she was old enough to earn. I'd no idea she was born and brought up here in Melbury, so when I was asked to take over at the mill of course I accepted. Even then she didn't say anything. But after a bit I spotted that there was something horribly wrong, she wasn't sleeping and had bad dreams and I caught her several times having a good cry over the sink. Then about a fortnight before we moved down here I got it out of her. She'd been trying to tell me, poor girl, but she hadn't been able to."

"And by then it was too late for you to back out and turn the job down."

"I offered, but she wouldn't hear of it, bless her. She said she didn't want to feel guilty about ruining my career on top of everything else. Then she came up with this idea of calling herself Eileen, which is her second name, and pretending she'd never been here before. I could see what her thinking was. She was coming back to a nightmare of a place where she'd blotted her copybook, and her relatives had been horrible to her and she couldn't face it. So she wanted to become a different person who hadn't had any of this happen to her, it would make things easier that way. I didn't think it would work, but she begged so hard that I went along with it, it was the least I could do for her."

"And unfortunately your visitor blew her cover," said Celia.

"Awful, wasn't it? I tried to put that pompous ass off in case he put his foot in it, he's the sort of man who would, but when he heard we'd got the Parish Council coming it made him even keener to do the honours himself. Barbara's horribly upset, but I've tried to make her see that it's not disastrous. She's still the wife of the manager at the mill, she can keep her distance and not see more of the rest of the family than she wants to. I've had a word about this with George Tunney and told him how she feels about the past. He quite understands, and I think he'll make them all behave sensibly."

"Oh good," said Celia. "The joker in the pack is her brother Simon. If anyone's going to make trouble, he will."

"I know. Simon's the real bogey man, she goes white if you even mention him."

"Really? I wonder why?"

"Don't ask her, will you? That was the whole idea of me coming here. She hopes you'll go on getting to know each other and planning her garden together, but that's only going to be possible if what we've just talked about is never mentioned again."

What a nice straightforward man, Celia thought when he

had gone, exactly right for a neurotic woman like his Barbara. The neuroses had probably stayed under control till the move to Melbury brought them to crisis point, but he was coping with them well.

For almost a week Celia could do nothing about Barbara because she was too busy with her stand for the July show at the Horticultural Hall. When the show was over, she rang her. Her call was welcomed ecstatically and she invited herself over for another planning session, at which they decided on intermediate irises rather than tulips to give colour early in the season. It was all very easy and friendly, and when they agreed to be on first name terms, Barbara even managed a nervous giggle about the collapse of the Eileen impersonation. But as they were deciding against a hedge of Frau Dagmar Hastrup roses as too liable to sucker, she suddenly broke off in mid-sentence. A scene on the far side of the mill-race had caught her attention, and seemed to horrify her.

Ted Bradshaw had just come out of the mill office, driving Simon Berridge in front of him. Simon was waving his arms wildly and shouting. A quarrel which had begun in the office seemed to be continuing, but the roar of the mill-race drowned their voices and made it impossible to hear what the argument was about. Presently they came to blows; or rather, Simon took a wild swipe at Bradshaw but missed, and Bradshaw gave him a push which sent him spinning. He got up again roaring with anger, but by then Bradshaw had gone back into his office and shut the door. Simon attacked it furiously. Finding it locked he went away, muttering angrily to himself, and disappeared round the corner of the building.

Barbara had watched her brother's antics with an expression of such disgust and hatred that it made Celia shiver. She longed to ask why Simon was such an outstanding figure of horror. It sounded as if Bradshaw knew the answer, but he had warned her not to put the question to Barbara, the whole subject was taboo. It seemed best to pretend that nothing abnormal had happened, so she tried to revive the debate over which rose to plant as a hedge. But it was no good, Barbara was too shaken, the relaxed mood could not be recaptured. The only sensible course was to make an excuse and leave.

Back at Archerscroft amusement reigned. The Tidmarshes' goat had embarked on an expedition down the lane, dragging behind it on the end of a long rope the tin bath to which it had been tethered. The Tidmarsh family was in hot pursuit, with the little girl in front screaming excitedly and egging the goat on.

"I dunno which is sillier," Bill muttered as the procession went past. "What's in front or them that's chasing along behind."

"We don't want to make enemies of the Tidmarshes," said Celia firmly, "so please don't say anything more to them about shooting the wretched creature."

"What'll I do then? Tell it to help itself when it comes busting in?"

"The Tidmarshes say they're going to put up a six-foot fence along our boundary."

"They been saying that for weeks, and there's still no sign or smell of it. And for why? They hired Simon Berridge to put it up for them."

"Him?" said Celia, shocked. "Oh no, how idiotic."

Simon Berridge maintained a vague claim to be a self-employed ditcher, fencer, rat-catcher and odd-job man, but only innocents like the Tidmarshes would have taken at face value his vivid description of how quickly and efficiently he would erect their six-foot fence. No one in the village would have trusted him to post a letter for them.

Celia thought for a little. "They'll have to be warned about Simon and told to get someone sensible on the job. I'll go round there later and see what I can do."

When she called on the Tidmarshes late in the afternoon, Simon Berridge was vaguely at work just inside the gate. He had assembled a few chestnut poles and some wire along the boundary with the nursery, but did not seem to be doing anything much with them. He treated Celia to a look of blazing honesty with his glass eye, and of hangdog furtiveness with the good one. The latter was explained when she saw that his fencing activities consisted of setting a rabbit snare in the hedge. She asked him if the Tidmarshes were at home.

"Let me see now. They was round at the back last time I see them, a-searchin' for the delicious free-range eggs what their hens lay in the hedges."

Deciding that the search would be in vain with Simon Berridge around, she went round to the back of the house and found Tidmarsh holding the head of the goat while his wife milked it.

"Ah, Mrs. Grant," he said. "We're sorry if our livestock has been intrusive, but Mr. Berridge is even now putting up a fence which will obviate any further difficulty."

"He isn't, you know," said Celia. "He's setting a rabbit snare in your hedge."

"A rabbit snare?" said Wendy Tidmarsh. "Oh no, you must be mistaken. Mr. Berridge is devoted to wild creatures, he told me so himself. He'd never dream of doing such a horrible, cruel thing."

Instead of answering, Celia went over to the boundary hedge and searched along it. "Here's another one."

Tidmarsh let go of the goat's head. It bounded away, upsetting the milkpail, and he came over to inspect her discovery. "Oh. Is that what they are? Wendy, Wendy! Mrs. Grant says the bits of wire we found in the hedge are rabbit snares."

"Oh no!" cried Wendy. "It's disgraceful, how could he?"

"I'm sorry," said Celia. "But someone has to tell you. Simon Berridge is a feckless ne'er-do-well who lives on his wife's earnings and social security. He drinks, and I don't think he's put up a fence in his life."

"Oh," said Tidmarsh. "Have we been taken in?"

"I'm afraid so."

"Right. We'll see about this." He strode off in fighting

mood and told Berridge loudly that he was a brutal oppressor of wild creatures and must never darken the Tidmarsh small-holding again. Berridge protested his innocence, but had to retreat before the torrent of reproach and began loading his fencing materials into his ramshackle little van.

"Those chestnut poles aren't tall enough," Celia told Wendy, "and he's not got enough of them to do a quarter of the job."

The shouting match took a new turn. Berridge, it seemed, had extorted a princely advance "to buy the posts and wire." Tidmarsh was insisting that he return the advance. Berridge, who had probably spent most of it already in the Red Lion, was refusing to do so, whereupon Tidmarsh tried to recoup himself in kind by preventing the removal of Berridge's inadequate supply of chestnut poles.

Celia took the opportunity to offer Wendy advice and help in devising an efficient tethering system for the goat, this being the ostensible purpose of her call.

"Oh no, please," said Wendy. "It's very kind of you, but you mustn't."

"Why not?"

"Keeping Gertrude under control is Edward's job. He'd be so humiliated if I called in outside help, it would make him feel inadequate."

As a goatherd he had every reason to feel inadequate, but Celia managed not to say so.

"I'm sorry," Wendy added, "but Edward's so terribly insecure and sensitive, I have to protect him all the time. If I let you interfere, it would put a tremendous strain on our marriage."

Celia brushed aside this claptrap. "I daresay, but something must be done. That goat is causing a lot of damage, and you're legally responsible."

"Oh dear, I'm sorry. I'll make sure he tethers it properly till we can get the fence put up. I will really, I promise."

Edward's battle with Simon Berridge had ended incon-clusively. He had managed to retain some of the fencing materials, but Berridge had driven off with at least half of the spoils.

"One has to be firm with that sort of person," said Edward with the air of one returning triumphant from the wars.

Celia was going to say something to him about the goat, but Wendy cut in quickly with, "Don't worry, I'll attend to it, I promise." With this Celia had to be content.

Bill Wilkins was even less content than she was when she reported back, and downright cross when Peter Verney looked in on his way home for another consultation about the ailing cyclamen. The first introduction of *Ambliseius mackenzii* had not produced any noticeable result, but Verney insisted that the cure would take time, and promised to bring another batch of them in a day or two as reinforcements.

"I still say we'd be better off with a good dose of Endrin," Bill grumbled.

"Then you'd have trouble with red spider and whitefly," said Verney. "Endrin would kill the predators that control them."

Bill muttered something subversive that sounded like "good riddance," and Celia, noting the pinched nostrils which heralded an explosion, ended the conference hastily.

"Oh, really Bill," she said when Verney had left, "I know you don't like him, but he's giving us the best advice on pest control we've had for years."

"I hate the slimy bugger, but that's nothing to do with it. All this messing about with insects gives me the bellyache."

He was clearly spoiling for a fight, but Celia cut him short and turned him out, on the grounds that she had to change for a dinner date. Bill withdrew to his cottage furious with her, and not just about Peter Verney and the insects. She was being far too soft with the Tidmarshes over the goat business, and he was worried about the possibility of sabotage at the nursery by the anonymous language-of-flowers correspondent who had threatened revenge for his rejection of her. That was Celia's fault, he had wanted to find out who it was and she had made it impossible.

He bolted his evening meal of cold meat and pickles in bad-tempered haste, and was beginning to feel the pangs of indigestion as he set off to the Red Lion. He would rather not have gone, but he had promised weeks ago to play in a darts team which had challenged the pub in a neighbouring village. The bar was crowded. George Tunney bought him a pint which he did not want, but would have to return in the next round, which also included George's policeman son Ron. Most of the darts team had already arrived: Charley Englefield from the village shop, Bob and Pat Pritchard, Chris Wood the postman, Andrew Berridge from the garage and several more players and supporters. Burchett was already in his usual observation post at the end of the bar.

Presently Simon Berridge wandered in to spend what remained of the Tidmarshes' money. Rolling his good eye wildly, he complained to anyone who would listen about their barbarous behaviour over his rabbit snares. "Ye'd think they'd thank me fer ridding them of the miserable little rodents, but oh no. 'Cruel to the dear little bunnies' they said."

This raised a general laugh. The village regarded the Tidmarshes as an uproarious joke.

Silence fell, and the darts match began. As a rule Bill was a reliable though not brilliant darts player, but tonight his eye was out and he made a mess of shot after shot. "Sorry," he muttered to Andrew Berridge, the captain. "I dunno what's wrong with me tonight."

His next few turns were fairly successful and he had hopes of recovering his form. But he missed a double-six which would have given the Melbury team the game, and stood by unhappily while the others tried in vain to retrieve his failure.

Presently the atmosphere of concentration was broken by Simon Berridge, who launched out into another beer-drenched catalogue of grievances, this time at the expense of the Bradshaws. They were his sister and brother-in-law, he argued, they owed it to him to give him the chance in life which he, poor orphan, had never had. But they had turned him away. Their hearts were of flint, and their water was thicker than their blood.

His listeners had no difficulty in decoding these confused remarks. Clearly, Simon had asked Bradshaw to promise him one of the jobs that would soon be going at the mill and Bradshaw, knowing his reputation, had refused. This time no one laughed, for he had broken ranks with the consensus about how the Bradshaws should be treated. One would pass the time of day with them if one met them in the street, but one would not claim relationship or make any reference to the past. The Bradshaws wanted to keep their distance, and that suited the village very well. Everyone agreed that sleeping dogs should be left to lie.

Bill missed part of what followed, because he had just been introduced to a supposedly expert gardener on the visiting team who babbled boringly about dahlias and vegetable marrows. But he overheard enough to grasp that Simon was not prepared to let sleeping dogs lie. He was threatening to rake up the ancient scandal about Barbara Berridge in front of a pubful of people, including the visiting darts team. His revelations were drowned in a chorus of anxious disapproval led by George and Ron Tunney, and the sinister Burchett, looking agitated, rose from his observer's stool at the end of the bar to intervene. The noise was distracting the darts players, and Ron Tunney broke off in the middle of his turn to cross the room with his confident policeman's tread and quell it. "Hold your noise now, Simon, you're disturbing the game."

Simon began to protest, but Ron took hold of him firmly by the lapels. "Sit down and shut your noise."

Cringing before his determined cousin, Simon subsided and sat mumbling under his breath till the end of the match. The result was a crushing defeat for Melbury, which was largely Bill's fault.

He was about to leave when Simon came lurching drunkenly towards him. "I got a bone ter pick with you."

"What's that then?"

"You was up my wife, you was," Simon shouted, loud enough for everyone to hear. "You been up her knickers, you dirty great blond fornicating turkey-cock of a Prince Charming."

Bill was utterly taken aback. "Who the hell told you this filthy fairy story?"

"T'ain't no fairy story," Simon shouted, addressing the bar at large. "My Joan confessed on her knees, she did, and begged me to fergive her. It weren't her fault, she resisted him with all her feeble strength, it was him forced himself on her in his filthy insane lust. On the table in the potting shed, she said, after the others had gone home. Twice."

Everyone in the bar was listening. Any slur on Bill's sexual morals made him see red, and the idea that he could have raped anyone, let alone fat, sleepy, moon-faced Joan Berridge was ridiculous. The sensible course would have been to laugh the thing off as a typical piece of drunken mischief-making by Simon. But at the best of times Bill would have found this difficult, and after his failure at darts, Celia's fixation with insects and the tiresomeness of the Tidmarshes' goat, restraint was impossible. He hit Simon hard on the chin and forced him against the wall, pummelling him.

"Hey, steady there," said Charley Englefield, and pulled Bill away.

"We'll have no fighting in my bar," shouted the landlord.

"Come outside then, Berridge, you lying little runt," Bill raged.

Ron Tunney took charge, as if this was happening on the motorway. "Come on now, let's break this up. Time you went home, Simon, we've had enough loose talk from you for one night. And you, Mr. Wilkins, calm down, do. You can see he's had too much, he's not responsible for what he's saying."

Two of the onlookers took Simon by the arms and frog-marched him out of the pub. Bill tried to follow, but Ron Tunney, Charley Englefield and Chris Wood held him fast.

"Let me go," he roared. "I'll learn him to talk filth about me."

He tried to struggle free, but it was three against one. When they let him go, he stormed out of the pub in a murderous rage to find Simon Berridge.

❧ THREE ❧

Peter Verney was driving home late. As he turned off the High Street into the lane leading to Archerscroft and his own house, his headlights picked out a man striding along in the middle of the road who took no notice of the car coming up behind him, but marched on, making it impossible to pass. Verney gave him a gentle toot on the horn. The man started, as if recalled from some absorbing train of thought, and moved aside towards the hedge. Driving past, Verney saw who it was: Bill Wilkins.

Wilkins was a problem, he decided, one that needed very sensitive handling. He was not just Celia Grant's head gardener, but a business confidant and close friend. How close, though? Close enough to block the development of any other personal relationship of hers that he disliked? Probably, and Wilkins obviously loathed his guts. But with luck and tact it might be possible to avoid an open breach. If one pretended to notice nothing, there was a hope that time and a friendly manner would bring him round.

As the car's headlights vanished ahead, Bill strode along down the lane, still in a murderous rage. His set-to with Simon Berridge had brought his indigestion to crisis point and he had vomited up the beer and his bolted evening meal into a hedge. Simon had a nerve, how dare he? As if Bill would dream of laying a finger on fat, moon-faced Joan Berridge in her granny-glasses, let alone rape her. It was a filthy thing to say, anything to do with casual sex was filthy. In front of a barful of gaping, dirty-minded locals too. Even they couldn't believe he was that kinky. Simon had probably intended it as some sort of malicious perverted joke, but it was not funny and he deserved everything he got.

None of his anger had dissipated when he reached Archerscroft, and he was brought up short on the doorstep of his cottage by another reason for bad temper. A noise down by the seedbeds suggested that an intruder had fallen over some metal object, probably a watering can, in the darkness. He fetched a flashlamp, investigated and found, as he expected, the Tidmarshes' goat, munching away at its favourite pasture, a bed of *Aster frikartii*. It was still tethered to the tin bath, but had not managed to pull the bath over the fence after it. The noise he had heard was caused by its attempts to do so.

Right, he decided, I'll soon deal with that, and went to fetch the shotgun he had bought a year ago to deal with a family of rabbits which had managed to penetrate Archerscroft's defences, and had multiplied alarmingly under a toolshed. He loaded it and returned to the scene to mete out justice. He hardly knew which infuriated him most, the wreckage of plants that had taken months of care to propagate and bring on to flowering size, the goat's complacent expression as it looked up from its feast into the beam of the flashlamp, or the Tidmarshes' idiocy. The furious passions of the evening boiled up in him again, and he let the abominable creature have both barrels between the eyes. It kicked up its legs and fell down amid the *Aster frikartii*, dead.

As he gazed down at it, lights went on next door and the Tidmarshes came surging out, carrying flashlamps. "Who's there?" called Edward Tidmarsh. "Someone has fired a gun, who is it?"

"Me," Bill shouted crossly. "And don't say you wasn't warned."

48

Wendy broke into a high wail of lamentation. "Gertrude isn't here! He's shot Gertrude."

"Is that true?" Edward demanded.

"Yes, why not? I warned you, but you never took a blind bit of notice. Fancy tying that thing on behind it, you might as well have tethered it to a teacup."

"But we put masses of bricks in the bath," Wendy protested.

"And they spilled over as it was dragged along, anyone in their senses would have known they would."

"Sadist! Murderer!" shrieked Wendy.

Bill ignored her. "D'you want your goat back now, or will you collect it in the morning?"

"We will have it now," said Edward with dignity.

It was surprisingly heavy. Bill hoisted it over the fence and it fell at Edward's feet.

"We will never forgive you for this barbaric act," he said, "and mark my words, we animal lovers know how to make life difficult for brutes like you."

"You get naughty with me, and you'll not know what hit you," Bill retorted and stomped away. But as he let himself into the cottage, he found himself thinking that shooting the goat had been a bit dodgy. The Tidmarshes might unleash extreme animal rights activists to take violent reprisals against him, and Celia would be furious. He tried to lash himself back into a frenzy of righteous anger, and it worked for a time. But as he lay awake brooding on his wrongs, he could no longer suppress an uncomfortable feeling that he had over-reacted grossly to the events of the evening. His threat to kill the goat if it intruded again had not been meant seriously, it was just a ploy to frighten the Tidmarshes into keeping it under proper control. And why hadn't he treated Simon's smutty little joke with the contempt it deserved, instead of losing his temper and running amok? By the time he managed to fall into an uneasy sleep, he had convinced himself that he had behaved very, very foolishly.

In the morning he braved Celia in her office to confess

about the goat and argue the toss with her as best he could. But she seemed to know the bad news already. She was wearing the grim look which meant that she was about to cut him up into tiny pieces and throw him into the incinerator.

She held out a handwritten note. "This was in the letter box when I arrived."

It was a demand for blood-money for the killing of one pedigree goat by "your half-mad employee who is not to be trusted with firearms."

"Half-mad is right," Celia snapped. "What got into you?"

"I was within me rights."

"No you weren't, I've just looked it up. The owner of livestock is responsible for fencing it in, and if an animal escapes and does damage to a neighbour's property, the neighbour can claim compensation. But he can't shoot the animal unless the damage is continuing and can't be prevented in any other way, which is why farmers are allowed to shoot dogs which are running wild and worrying their sheep. There's nothing in the act which allows people like you with a grievance against life to take it out on animals as well as people."

Bill was startled. "What d'you mean, 'taking it out on people'?"

"What I say. Ever since Anthea was killed*, you've been shutting yourself up behind a wall of bad temper and barking at anyone who comes near you."

"But Celia, you feel let down when a thing like that happens. Anyone would."

"I daresay, but you ought to be over it by now, instead of which you're getting worse. Take this affair of the goat, I'd no idea you seriously intended to shoot it. I thought you were trying to frighten the Tidmarshes into keeping it under control, and I didn't even approve of that."

Bill retreated into a sullen silence. He had not "seriously

---

*See *Flowers of Evil*, 1987

intended" to shoot the goat, it had been a bad-tempered impulse. But he was not going to confess that to Celia.

"Anyway, thanks to you," she said, "I shall have to disgorge four hundred pounds which we can ill spare to the Tidmarshes, less seventy-five which is my counter-claim for the damage done by their goat."

"Four hundred pounds for a scruffy, smelly goat? They must be raving."

"Raving or not, I'm going to pay it, we can't afford to make our relations with them even worse by haggling. Now let's get down to business. Joan Berridge phoned just now in a frightful state, she won't be coming in today. Her husband hasn't been home all night and she's worried about him."

"I saw him last night in the Red Lion," said Bill, skating dodgily over a whole chapter of the evening's events. "Up to his ears in brown ale, he was. Still sleeping it off under a hedge, I bet."

"If I was Joan I'd tell him he could go and live under a hedge for good, but there's no accounting for tastes. Now, Bill, let's go and see what's happening to all those unfortunate cyclamen."

As far as she could see, there was little change. "But Peter said it would take time."

In Bill's opinion the infestation was getting worse. Why had she made him mess about with Verney's stuff instead of doing the job properly with an insecticide? After the bollocking she had just given him he was not going to argue and get into more trouble. So he followed her in sulky silence down to the seedbeds, where they worked side by side and furious with each other for most of the morning, without exchanging an unnecessary word.

Towards midday a call from Ann Hammond came through on the cordless telephone that Celia carried round the nursery with her; Simon Berridge had been found drowned in the river, half a mile below the mill-race.

"Horrors, Ann, what a tragedy," said Celia. "At least

I suppose it is, though some wives would regard it as a merciful release.''

"Joan doesn't, she's here at the surgery in a frightful state. She asked me to ring and say she won't be in for the rest of the week.''

When Celia told Bill the news a wave of unease hit him in the stomach. But he swallowed it back.

"I shan't call in on Joan to sympathise till tomorrow,'' she decided, "when she'll have had time to get over the first shock.''

"Oh Celia,'' Bill blurted out, "there's something I better tell you before you go to see Joan. Berridge and I had a bit of a shindy last night in the Red Lion.'' He told her about Simon's drunken accusation of rape. "He made it up to annoy me, it was his idea of a joke.''

"And did you treat it as a bad joke and ignore him? No, in your present bloody-minded state you probably worked yourself up into a frenzy and hit him on the nose.''

"You'd blow your top if someone called you a nasty name in front of a barful of people.''

"Probably, but I hope I'd have a controlled explosion and deal with it more sensibly. The punch on the nose happened inside the pub, did it? And then I suppose the landlord read the riot act and you invited Berridge to come outside for a manly bout of fisticuffs.''

"He went out and when I got away I looked for him, but he'd hid somewhere and I never found him. He was dead drunk, Celia. He must have wandered about and fell in the water.''

"But what was he doing down by the river?'' Celia objected. "It's a mile away from the Red Lion, in the opposite direction to his house.''

There was an uneasy silence as they both realised that wild rumours must be flying round the village already. Some of them would probably be translated into unpleasant suggestions at the inquest.

"What did Berridge actually say about you?'' Celia asked.

"That I'd raped his fat slob of a wife twice, on the potting-shed table. And then there was a great hush, right through the bar. Those men are dirty-minded, they believed it, see?"

"Not necessarily. I expect they were just curious. Your sex life leaves no visible trace in the shape of a girl friend, but anyone as dishy as you ought to be wallowing in an endless orgy of sexual prosperity. They must wonder all the time what you get up to and whether it's kinky. I agree that the village's collective mind is on the dirty side. But even they can't believe that what you really enjoy is raping grossly obese women in glasses."

"Then why did Berridge have to make up a story like that?"

"He didn't."

"He did, you should have heard him."

"No. It was Joan that made the story up and fed it to him."

"Why would she do that then?"

"To annoy and embarrass you. She was your language-of-flowers correspondent. Your snooty reply made her furious, and this is her revenge."

"You're saying it was her sent me them scatty bunches? How d'you know that?"

"I made it my business to find out."

"You never told me though."

"Of course not, you'd have made mincemeat of her and she'd have walked out on her job in tears. But of course I watched her, I was afraid her revenge for being a woman scorned would entail sabotaging the nursery. Accusing you of rape instead was rather ingenious."

"But Celia, why would Joan Berridge send me little love-messages? She must know she's nobody's sex-symbol, I thought it must be one of the packing-shed girls. You sure it's her?"

"Absolutely. The heliotrope was the clue, there's not a lot of it grown round here and I couldn't make out where anyone could have got hold of a bit. But that front garden of the Hawkinses, in Summerfield Close, which they've

53

tricked out so nastily with bedding plants, has a heliotrope as prize exhibit bang in the middle of it and it's only four doors down from the Berridges'. So I had a gossip with them over the hedge about how to propagate heliotrope. They grew it from seed, and didn't believe it would strike easily from cuttings. In the end it came out that someone had asked for a few bits to see if it could be done and they'd handed over some, saying 'you'll be lucky.' Needless to say, this optimistic person turned out to be our Joan.''

"She must be ripe for the madhouse, silly horny creature.''

"She isn't exactly mad, but I've been watching her and a lot goes on behind those glasses and that moon face that you wouldn't suspect. When she thinks people aren't looking she talks to herself under her breath. I'm pretty sure there are Walter Mitty-style fantasies going on inside there the whole time, passionate love affairs with film and telly stars and so on, and she reads Barbara Cartland over her sandwiches in the lunch hour. You obviously qualify as a fantasy lover, and her thing about you spilled over into the language-of-flowers business.''

"I still say she's mad if she thought her scatty bunches would make it with me for real.''

"She didn't. You weren't meant to know who they were from, let alone answer her. She got an answer she didn't like, and it brought the whole fantasy structure crashing down in ruins. When that happens to a person whose inner life is one long fantasy, it shatters their whole personality. They suddenly see themselves for what they are, and they panic and turn savage. Has she spread this rape story all round the village, I wonder?''

"I bet she has,'' said Bill savagely.

"Well that doesn't mean she'll be believed. And as for the other thing, we'll just have to hope that someone saw Berridge reeling about on his way to the river after you'd slaughtered the Tidmarshes' goat and retired to bed with the sense of an evening well spent.''

* * *

Wild rumours flew round the village for two days. Then Detective-Inspector Ferris from the Welstead CID presented himself at Archerscroft and asked to speak to "a Mr. Wilkins who I understand is employed here."

Celia did not like the look of Inspector Ferris, a sandy-haired man with an over-eager, foxy cast of face. She fetched Bill, who disliked him even more but took him into the kitchen of his cottage for the interview. "So what can I do for you then?"

"I'm investigating the death of Simon Francis Berridge, who was found dead in the river on Tuesday, and I hope you can help me with my enquiries."

"Not a lot. He was in the Red Lion Monday night, had a right old skinful too. He could have fell in the gutter on his way home, only he had bad luck, it was the river instead."

"I believe you and Berridge had an argument," said Ferris mildly. "Just before you left the pub."

"That's right. Accused me of having raped his wife, he did. It was a load of nonsense, but I'm strict in me morals, and I won't have them things said about me, so I blew me top."

"And you'd had a drink or two, no doubt?"

"Not much, I dropped out of the round after me second pint. I was playing in a darts match and I had to watch it."

"I see. And had you heard of this accusation of rape before Berridge came out with it in the pub?"

"No, it took the wind right out of me. I thought it was some nasty kind of joke."

"I'm told that during the darts match you seemed upset, and were playing well below your usual form. This wasn't because you already knew about this accusation against you?"

"No! I told you, it was the first I'd heard of it. I was properly taken aback."

Ferris paused, with a look of suppressed eagerness, like a fox stalking a chicken.

"Now Mr. Wilkins," he said. "I'd like you to tell me

in your own words what happened when you and Mr. Berridge left the Red Lion.''

"That's easy. When I blew me top the landlord said he wasn't having no fighting in his bar, so I said come outside. But the others who was there thought Simon had had enough of a bashing, so two of the lads marched him out and some of the others tried to keep me from following. But I got away and went to look for him, up and down the road, but there was no sign. I think the lads must have hid him so I wouldn't find him and give him another dose, and in the end I give up and went home.''

"So according to you, that was the last you saw of Berridge?''

"That's right.''

"Does it surprise you to hear that Berridge's wife says different? According to her, you and Berridge were in their front garden later that night, and you were bashing him about.''

Bill gaped. "What's that? Come again.''

Ferris repeated his remark and added, "She says it ended with Berridge chasing off down the road to get away, and you going after him. Want to alter what you said just now?''

"No. She's lying.''

"Is she, Wilkins, or are you?'' Ferris rasped, switching on the hostility. "You had a grudge against him, you lost track of him outside the Red Lion, so what did you do next? You waited for him outside his home and attacked him when he got there.''

"I never, it's a pack of lies.'' Gathering his wits, Bill began fighting back. "What time was all this supposed to happen?''

"A bit before eleven, she says.''

"I was back here by half after ten.''

"Prove it, can you?''

"Yes, I bloody well can. I had an argument with the neighbours over the fence.''

"At half past ten at night?''

56

"Their goat had broken into the nursery and was doing damage."

"So you got them up and made them take the animal away?"

"No. I shot it."

"You *shot* it? Going a bit far, weren't you?"

"It was always breaking in. I'd told them I would if it happened again."

Ferris hissed irritably between his teeth. "So this is the picture we get. You were upset for some reason we don't know about during the darts match, and played badly. Then Berridge tells this story of his and gets you in a foul temper. According to you, you go straight home, but you're still in a foul temper and you shoot the neighbour's goat—which, incidentally, you had no legal right to do. That's your version, but Mrs. Berridge doesn't agree with it. She says you were beating up her husband on their doorstep a bit before eleven, and you say you were back here by then, so it's a question of timing, right? If she's, say, fifteen minutes out, or you are, you'd have time to look in on Summerfield Close on your way home."

"It's not on me way home. It's a mile the other side of the Red Lion from here. I'd need a helicopter."

"Then what's your explanation, Wilkins?"

"I just told you. She's lying. She has a grudge against me."

"What sort of a grudge?"

Bill explained about Joan's language-of-flowers approaches to him, his angry reply and her threat of vengeance. "This is her way of getting back at me, see?"

"Bunches of flowers?" Ferris echoed, sounding disgusted at being told anything so fanciful. "Did anyone see them besides you?"

"Yes, Mrs. Grant did, who runs the nursery."

"I'll check with her, and I'll have a word with your neighbours about the timing of the episode with the goat. But I'll want to come back to you, so don't leave the neighbourhood without letting Welstead police station know."

"What is all this then? He was drunk. He fell in the river. You've no call to go at me like this."

"That's where you're wrong, Wilkins. There was no water in his lungs. According to the medical evidence he died from a heavy blow to the head that cracked his skull, and he was put in the water after he was dead."

There was a tense silence. After some concentrated thought Bill said, "So what you've cooked up is this: I give him a bashing in Summerfield Close a bit before eleven, then I carry him two miles on me back because I don't have me car with me, and I put him in the river. And when I get back here it's still only half past ten."

"Half past ten is what you say. Others may say different."

Indeed they might, Bill thought with a pang of anxiety. The Tidmarshes would be in no mood to confirm his alibi after his massacre of their goat.

"Well, that'll be all for the present," said Ferris. "I'll check with your neighbours about the timing of that goat business, but first I'll have a word with your Mrs. Grant about those bunches of flowers you say you had from Mrs. Berridge."

Celia confirmed the story of the love-posies, but that did not satisfy Ferris. "What evidence have you, madam, that it was Mrs. Berridge who sent them?"

She told him about the heliotrope in the front garden of the council house four down from the Berridges. "And the Hawkinses say she asked them for a cutting. I think that's conclusive."

"I'm not a gardener myself, madam, but would you say this heliotrope's a rare plant?"

"Not really. It's one of those old-fashioned things that people don't bother with much, probably because it's a bit fiddly. It needs over a year in a glasshouse to grow from seed to flowering size."

"But there are other possible sources besides the front garden at Mrs. Berridge's neighbour's?"

"I suppose so, yes."

"And when Mrs. Berridge asked them for a bit, it doesn't follow that she wanted it to put in the bunch of flowers for your Mr. Wilkins. She could have intended to grow it as a cutting."

"Of course. Why don't you ask her?"

Ferris made no comment on this suggestion. "Would you say Mr. Wilkins was a steady young man?"

"Yes. He's been with me for five years and he's absolutely reliable."

"I meant in his personal life."

"I don't think he has one, not since his girl friend died two years ago. He hasn't got over it, and I'm sure he doesn't go in for casual sex. In fact he disapproves of it strongly."

"Uptight about sexual matters then?"

"I didn't say that. Is Joan Berridge still peddling that ridiculous story about him raping her? Because if so, I wouldn't take any notice, she spends her days in a fog of self-generated romantic fiction."

"Rape's not romantic, Mrs. Grant."

"I know, but what would a man with Bill Wilkins' looks want with a lump like Joan Berridge?"

"It doesn't follow. Teenage louts do it to women in their seventies and eighties. What did Mr. Wilkins' girl friend die of?"

Celia had hoped this question would not arise. But there was no help for it, so she told him. "She was shot."

"By accident?"

"No. On purpose, by a man who owed her money. It upset Bill dreadfully."

"I see. There must be a police record of this episode. Where did it happen?"

"At Glyndebourne, near Lewes."

"Thank you. And the young woman's name?"

"Anthea Clarkson. Do check up, but you'll find that Bill Wilkins had nothing to do with what happened, he was a completely innocent party."

When Ferris had gone, Bill told Celia about Joan Berridge's claim to have seen him attacking Simon outside their house.

"Bill, listen carefully. You told me the last you saw of Simon Berridge was when he walked out of the Red Lion. Is that true?"

"Oh yes, Celia. I swear." He was looking her straight in the eye, but soon found that he could not face her steady gaze. "It's true, but there's something dodgy I never told you and I should have."

"Yes, Go on."

"After I been looking around for a bit outside the Red Lion and finding no sign or smell of him, I thought, this is no good, I'll go up to Summerfield Close and wait for him to come home and give him a bit of me mind there. So I stood about a bit in their front garden, but there was still no sign of him, so I thought, what if he's home already, shall I knock? And then it come to me, if I knock and he's not there and his great fat wife is, what'll I look like seeing she's accused me of raping her? So I come away again, and I was back here at half past ten like I told that bastard Ferris."

"But you didn't tell him you'd been to Summerfield Close?"

"No. I never."

"Bill, you idiot. Suppose someone saw you there? You must tell Ferris at once before they do."

"Okay, Celia. But it don't matter much one way or the other. I could never have put Simon in the river and got back here by half past ten."

Celia's face was grim. "Bill, if you did lose your temper with Simon and hit him too hard I want you to tell me. I'll do my best for you, and we can prove that you didn't mean to kill him. But I couldn't bear it if you told me a lie."

"I'm not lying, Celia. I'd never lie to you."

"Good. I've heard your version of what happened, and I believe it." She sighed. "Oh dear, this is partly my fault. I should never have made you send a rude answer to her love-posies. I shattered her girlish dream about you and this is the result.''

"Oh Celia, you weren't to know. Silly cow, fancy accusing me of killing Simon. You'd think she'd done enough mischief already with her rape nonsense.''

"I'll have to go and condole with her tomorrow. Perhaps I can make her see some sense. Anyway, I'll try.''

Meanwhile Detective-Inspector Ferris was pursuing his enquiries at the Tidmarshes', in a kitchen which smelt strongly of herbs and unsuccessful brews of home-made wine.

"He was in a dreadful state,'' said Wendy Tidmarsh, "shouting and swearing at us.''

"Had he been drinking, in your opinion?'' Ferris asked.

"Oh, I think he must have. Only a tipsy person would take out his bad temper on a poor dumb animal.''

"And when did all this happen, Mrs. Tidmarsh?''

There was some hesitation about this, but after a hint from Ferris, Wendy exclaimed, "I remember now! Wasn't that the night we listened to that BBC science programme? The one about the frightful risks the scientists were taking with genetic engineering?''

Edward hesitated for a moment, then agreed. "It's a subject of enormous concern to environmentalists, so we stayed up late specially.''

"And we heard the shots just after it finished,'' said Wendy.

Ferris asked when the programme ended, and Wendy handed him the *Radio Times*. He opened it at the television programmes.

"It was on radio,'' she said loftily. "We don't bother with television.''

Ferris turned the page to the radio schedule and read: *Science today: A revolution in the protection of commercial food crops is just round the corner, as experimenters with genetic engineering produce viruses which attack plant pests and diseases. But is enough being done to ensure that mutated viruses which might be dangerous are not released into the environment*? The programme was scheduled to end at ten minutes to twelve.

"Well thank you," said Ferris happily. "That's what I wanted to know."

When he returned to the Berridges' he found Joan sitting in state in her front room, surrounded by excited sympathisers. He expelled them, and began questioning her again. "You're sure it was Wilkins you saw out there attacking your husband?"

"Yes." She was very nervous. The flat moon face was pink and the eyes behind her steel-rimmed glasses constantly shifted focus.

"Wilkins says it wasn't him."

"Well, he would say that, wouldn't he?" she managed after a severe intellectual effort.

"Could you have made a mistake? It was dark out there, the moon's in the first quarter."

"No!" she cried. "Oh no, I couldn't have. The light was on in the kitchen and the curtains wasn't drawn. When I heard the noise I went up to the bedroom and looked out. I could see him in the light from the kitchen window, clear as I see you now."

"Well, thank you, Mrs. Berridge. Now there's something else I have to put to you. Mr. Wilkins says that someone has been leaving small bunches of flowers as love-tokens, sort of, in his kitchen for him to find. He claims that it was you left them there."

"Flowers? Love-tokens for Mr. Wilkins?" she echoed in alarm. "I never, what d'you mean?"

Ferris explained again. In increasing panic she told him she knew nothing about it, it was nothing to do with her.

He glanced round the room. The window-sill held a display of potted plants which gave evidence of her green-fingered skill. "There's a flower called heliotrope," he said, "d'you grow it?"

She brightened at once. "I've tried. A neighbour gave me some cuttings, but I didn't manage to strike them. There's one not quite dead yet, I'll get it and show you."

She went out, and came back with a small flowerpot containing a stick with a few wizened leaves still attached to it. "I think it's the wrong time of year."

"So if anyone says you obtained a piece of this heliotrope from a neighbour so that you could put it in one of these posies for Mr. Wilkins, that would be wrong?"

Suddenly her large frame was shaken by tears. "Of course it's wrong. I hate him, and you know why."

"Ah yes. About this accusation of rape, you didn't complain at the time and it's a bit late to proceed against him. But you could get him for sexual harassment at work if you've a mind to."

"No, no, I wouldn't want to do that."

Wondering why not, Ferris went back to police headquarters in Welstead and fed a request for information about Bill Wilkins' dead girl friend Anthea Clarkson into his computer terminal. There was only a bare mention of Wilkins in the summary of the case, so next morning he rang Lewes for more details. These were so interesting that he decided to put the frighteners on Wilkins by summoning him for a formal interview and telling the press that "a man was helping them with their enquiries" into the death of Simon Berridge. He let Wilkins stew for twenty minutes in the passage, then confronted him across the desk in a bleak interview room, with a constable present to take notes.

"Now, Wilkins, we're going right through it again, and this time I want the truth and not a lot of fancy stuff about bunches of flowers and such. According to Mr. and Mrs. Tidmarsh, you shot their goat shortly before twelve, not at half past ten like you said. Better change your story, hadn't you?"

"No."

"Why not?"

"Because my story's right. The Tidmarshes got it wrong."

"No they bloody didn't. They were listening to a science programme on the radio, something to do with genetic en-

63

gineering, they said. It finished at ten to twelve, and they heard the shots shortly after that.''

''They're lying then. I shot their goat, and they're getting their own back on me.''

''So. Anyone who tells a different story from what you do is lying because they have a grudge against you, is that right?''

Bill said nothing. Hatred for his foxlike persecutor welled up in him, but he knew he must keep his cool, otherwise he would get confused and make a mess of this intricate game of verbal chess. With an enormous effort of will, he managed not to blow his top.

''Another thing,'' Ferris went on. ''Mrs. Berridge says she knows nothing about those love-posies you say she sent you.''

''But she begged some heliotrope off of a neighbour to put in one of them.''

''No. It was because she wanted to try growing some for herself from cuttings. She showed me one, half dead in a pot.''

Bill's head was perfectly clear as he considered his answer. ''I'm not surprised. The cuttings wouldn't strike in July, it's the wrong time of year. Joan's good with plants, she'd know that, well as I do.''

''So?''

''So she begs a lot of shoots from the Hawkinses and sends one of them to me. Then she pots up the rest so everyone would think she wanted them for that.''

Suddenly Ferris began to shout. ''You can explain bloody everything, can't you? Everyone's against you, they're all out to do you down. Paranoia, that's what it's called, it's a well-known mental disease. But you haven't got it, you're shamming. Hoping to be remanded for a psychiatric report, is that it?''

''Have to get me into court first, won't you?'' Bill suggested, gazing at him calmly. A phoney burst of anger to break the suspect down was a stock policeman's trick, but Ferris seemed to be losing his cool for real. His hands trembled, and a muscle was twitching at the side of his jaw. He pushed back his chair with a jarring noise and strode tensely round the room, clenching his fists so that the knuckles showed white.

Presently he sat down again and remarked in a calmer tone, "You're a bit uptight about sex, I'm told."

"Who says?"

"Information received. No girl friend that anyone knows of. Boys?"

"No. Don't talk dirty."

"Everything about sex is dirty, is that right?"

"No. Not when you're going steady with a girl you're fond of."

"I been wondering about that. When a fine upstanding young man like you doesn't have a girl friend, people ask themselves what goes on."

"My steady died."

"Yes. Anthea Clarkson, I know all about her. Let you down properly, didn't she? So we get a picture of a girl who drugs her employer and sells his trade secrets to a rival firm. When she gets caught out doing that and blackmailed, she kills her blackmailer. In the end a fellow-criminal kills her because she asks for her slice of the money and he hasn't got it to give her. Now, Wilkins. I ask myself how her boy friend is going to react when his eyes are opened and he finds himself looking into this can of worms. He's going to be disgusted and turn against all women, isn't he?"

"No. He just doesn't trust people so easy afterwards, that's all."

"And he gets very uptight about sex."

"Let's say he doesn't rush into anything else in a hurry, it's natural. He hasn't found anyone yet that he wants to go steady with."

"So what happens? Kerb-crawling? Pick-ups and one-night stands?"

"None of that. I'm fussy."

"Uptight," Ferris corrected. "No normal healthy outlet

for it, is there? Let's talk now about what you did to Mrs. Berridge.''

"I didn't do nothing to her, she made it up."

"So you say."

"Look at it this way, is it likely? If I'd wanted a woman just to relieve meself with, I'd only have to lift me little finger. I've had the come-on from all sorts, not just girls with no sense and no morals, but respectable-seeming wives too, fine-looking women some of them. With all that lot keen to oblige, why would I bother with an ugly great mass of blubber like Joan Berridge?"

"If you'd dealt with it as often as I have, you'd know looks don't come into it over rape, not as a rule. There's no question of sexual attraction. Old ladies get raped, ugly women too, much uglier than your Mrs. Berridge. Your typical rapist is a repressed man with no normal sexual outlet, who hates women because of something in his past and can't relate to them normally. He does it out of hate, it's a sort of revenge for whatever it was that turned him against women, like you after Anthea Clarkson let you down with a great big bump. You're not just a plausible liar, Wilkins. You're a pervert.''

At long last, Bill lost his cool. Ferris had stuck his chin out invitingly as he made his accusation, and Bill hit it hard.

❧ FOUR ❧

In due course Celia paid her delayed visit of condolence to Joan Berridge, and was received in state in the front room. But her attempt to batter some sense out of her fat, half-demented employee got nowhere. Joan was surrounded by a guard of honour of female relatives, for whose benefit she was staging a tremendous carry-on of widowly lamentation for her worthless Simon. She could not be brought to the point, and merely sobbed at Celia from behind a sopping handkerchief whenever she was asked anything awkward. Celia longed to give her a short sharp shaking and make her confess that her allegations against Bill of rape and murder came straight out of the melting-pot of her over-heated imagination. But her queries had already provoked a restive movement among the relatives, who clearly thought them out of place during a visit of condolence. At the risk of being thrown out for improper behaviour, she put a direct question about the alleged rape. Joan's only answer was to sob even louder.

"But Joan, you know Mr. Wilkins would never do anything like that, why are you saying he did?"

"Berridge misunderstood," she murmured between two outbursts.

"Misunderstood what?"

67

"What I told him."

This was too much for the relatives. Before Celia could ask what she had told Berridge, a woman Celia had never seen before that morning, with a sharp nose, a white face and very black hair, stood up and said, "She's not fit to answer all these questions, surely you can see? And I don't know what business they are of yours anyway." So saying she started marching Joan tenderly but firmly out of the room. "Come, dear. You'll feel better if you have a lie down."

Joan treated Celia to a woebegone backward look from the doorway. Her blubbery lips moved, as if she was about to speak. But the sharp-nosed woman gave her a tug and she let herself be led away.

Wondering what the look meant, Celia went back home, and found Bill sitting on the doorstep waiting for her. As she walked up the path he rose stiffly and limped painfully towards her.

"Bill! Good heavens, what on earth's happened to you?"

"I was beat up at the police station."

"Horrors. Come in and I'll get you a drink."

The beating up had been cleverly done, for his face had been left untouched. But he was obviously in great pain, caused, he said, by bruises round his ribs and stomach. She brought him a stiff whisky, then asked him what had happened. His blow-by-blow account of his interrogation by Ferris sounded as if he had kept his temper and handled it well, and she said so.

"That's right, I kept my cool. Right till near the end."

"Then what happened?"

"I hit Ferris and they started in on me, him and the other chap that was there with a notebook, one of them holding me against the wall while the other one hit me. When they'd finished, Ferris said if I made a complaint they'd do me for assaulting the police."

"But Bill, what was it made you lose your cool?"

"He'd found out all about me and Anthea. He reckoned because I hadn't found meself another girl after she died,

I must be a pervert with a hang-up about straight sex, and that's why I'd gone and raped Joan Berridge. Silly mad cow, why did she have to make up a story like that?"

Celia groaned. "I don't think she's grasped that one should keep one's girlish dreams to oneself when the police ask questions about a murder."

"Oh Celia, you couldn't go there and see if you can get some sense out of her?"

"I've just been. All I got was a lot of defensive boo-hooing from behind a very wet handkerchief, but I'll try again when she's had time to calm down."

"And the Tidmarshes been telling Ferris lies too, they say it was near on midnight when we had the argument about the goat."

"Horrors, that wrecks your alibi. Had you told him you went looking for Simon earlier at his house, and came away?"

"No, and after that I decided not to, it was too dodgy."

"Quite right, damn the Tidmarshes. Revenge for the goat, I suppose. Dear me, what a mess."

"Celia, you couldn't talk to them too, see if you can make them behave reasonable?"

"I'll try." She had little hope of success, but did not say so for fear of the effect on Bill's already low morale. She offered to cook dinner for them both, but he seemed to want to be alone with his misery.

"Oh Celia, thank you. But I'm that shook up I couldn't eat a thing. If you'll excuse me, I think I'd best be off home to get me head down. Being beat up by the police is very exhausting, and I been sleeping badly these days."

He went, assuring her that he was perfectly all right really, just very tired. His departure left her with a blank, for she always talked over her problems with him and she had one now. Who else was there? Obviously, Peter Verney. She rang him and invited him in for a drink.

He was with her from next door within minutes, and she put her problem to him: how did one begin to understand the behaviour of a woman like Joan Berridge, whose mental processes were obviously chaotic? "She must fantasise all the time, how can anyone cope with all that going on in their head?"

"Oh, I do see the difficulty. You have to remember to put out the empty milk bottles while you're panting in the hot embraces of a Bedouin chief."

"Yes, but what happens when the hot embraces and the milk bottles get so mixed up that you think it's all happening in real life? You send real flowers to Bill, who is your fantasy lover. And thanks to my stupidity you get a rude herbaceous put-down from him. Collapse of fantasy. Your loved one has rejected you, he's shown you to yourself as you really are, a fat middle-aged woman married to a drunken layabout who expects you to do the bread-winning as well as the housework. So what's the next step?"

"Revenge," Peter suggested. "She tells her husband that Wilkins raped her. For good measure she adds that Wilkins and Berridge had a fight to the death in her front garden."

"As fantasy it makes perfect sense. Two admirers fighting about you, delicious."

"And you're Helen of Troy, watching from the battlements."

"Exactly, but what about the real life aspect?"

A silence fell, as they circled round the awkward issue that had to be faced next.

"I've only met Wilkins once or twice," said Verney, "and you've known him for years. What do you think?"

"He wouldn't lie to me, if he'd attacked Simon as she said, he'd tell me. I'm absolutely certain of that."

"Even if he'd cracked Berridge's skull and dumped him in the river?"

Celia hesitated. "When Bill's in a temper, he's quite capable of hitting a man so hard that it kills him. But he would have behaved quite differently afterwards. He'd realise at once that dumping Simon in the river wouldn't be a good idea, policemen who found the corpse with a cracked skull in the water wouldn't take easily to the idea that it had drowned itself. He'd also realise that when it was found,

70

he'd be the prime suspect after his very public quarrel with Simon in the Red Lion. He'd leave the corpse where it was and tell the police that he'd hit Simon rather harder than he meant to under great provocation, and hadn't intended to kill him. His next action would have been to tell me the whole story.''

Peter put his hand on hers, and she did not withdraw it. ''I accept that absolutely,'' he said. ''This is horrible for you, I realise that. If there's anything I can do—''

''You're being enormously helpful already, it's such a relief to have someone objective to talk it over with. Where have we got to?''

''Wilkins is innocent and we're back at Joan Berridge making wild accusations of rape.''

''I think she may not have gone as far as that.''

''Oh? Why not?''

''Because the only coherent remark I got out of her was 'Berridge misunderstood.' That could mean that she consoled herself for her disappointment by fantasising about some sort of tender sexual approach by Bill, and got herself into such a state that she said something about it to Simon. And Simon, being the sort of man he was, decided it made a better story if he hyped it up into rape.''

''Or alternatively,'' Peter argued, ''she told him that Bill had raped her. And when she's confronted with you, she comes down to earth with a bump and realises that this isn't the way to ingratiate oneself with one's employer. So she pretends to you that she told him nothing of the kind.''

''That's possible too. Whichever way it is, 'Berridge misunderstood' means she'd like to go back on the story. But Simon has gone public with it, and she's stuck with it as far as the village is concerned. The censorship clamped down the moment she began to back-track.''

''Interesting,'' said Verney. ''Who are these women mounting guard?''

''Kathleen Tunney and Ada Berridge from the garage and Mrs. Englefield and Mrs. Perkins, née Tunney and Berridge respectively. Very much a family affair, except that the

71

censor-in-chief was a tall woman with dyed black hair who I've never seen before in my life. They seemed to be there to keep her on the rails and make sure she told her story without getting into a muddle.''

"And the story includes an allegation that Wilkins bashed Simon about in their front garden," said Peter. "What an imagination the woman has.''

"I suspect that someone did give Simon a bashing out there," said Celia. "But it wasn't Bill.''

"Then the obvious scenario goes something like this. Simon is attacked outside the Berridges' house by X, who runs down the road after him, kills him, and dumps him in the river. The police say it isn't a case of drowning. This is awkward, because Joan has seen X, so she must be squared. Wilkins, who has had a very public quarrel with Simon, is the obvious fall guy. So Joan is told to say it was Wilkins she saw.''

"That's right," said Celia. "She's a woman scorned, and she wants to get even with Bill, so she plays along very willingly. She is also encouraged by X to stick firmly to the rape story, because it helps to blacken Bill in the eyes of the police.''

"Next problem," said Verney. "Who is X? Someone else who quarrelled with Simon and gave him a bashing and panicked when he found he'd bashed too hard?''

"Or a cold and calculating murderer," Celia suggested, "who realises that this is the moment to strike, he's been handed it on a plate. Bill losing his temper with Simon has provided him with a fall guy if things go wrong.''

"Then your murderer must have been in the Red Lion that evening. Otherwise he wouldn't know about the Berridge–Wilkins row. Why does he want to murder Simon?''

She thought about this. "Goodness knows. The village presents a united front to the likes of us, but they do a lot of in-fighting among themselves. Half a dozen people could have a motive. Goodness, look at the time! You'll stay for a scratch supper?''

"May I? I'd love to, I was resigning myself to the clammy remains of yesterday's cold pork pie."

They discussed the problem some more over lamb cutlets and a crisp salad, but without getting anywhere. After he had gone, Celia tried for a time to drug herself with late night television. But fictitious policemen and criminals were behaving brutally on all the channels which were not reporting real-life brutality in Palestine or Northern Ireland, so she went to bed. When sleep did not come, she switched on the light again and began to read a learned article about the distribution in China and the Far East of ten distinct species of *Adenophora*. This proved boring enough to promote sleep, and she was about to switch off the light when the telephone rang.

"Oh Celia, can't you sleep either? Saw your light on down the lane and thought I'd ring."

"How are you now, Bill?"

"A bit stiff but okay, I had a good sleep and woke up an hour ago. Listen, I got an idea. Something that happened that night in the Red Lion."

"Good. Tell me."

"It was during the darts match. A lot of us was waiting our turn to play and Simon came weaving across to the bar in a great pother about a grievance he had on his mind. It was the Bradshaws he was on about, how they was hard as flints, and they'd turned him away when he asked them for help, although he was their relation, and how they'd left him to starve, but he'd get even with them. Well, soon as he started on this, Charley Englefield and Chris Wood began to shush him, and that spying butler of the colonel's joined in, and Andrew Berridge took me away in a hurry to meet a man in the visiting team who was supposed to be a very expert gardener. Well the chap was nice but nothing special, dahlias and vegetable marrows and such, it was an excuse, see, so I shouldn't hear any more—but I did a bit, while I was being took away. Simon was saying how Paul Templewood wasn't the father of his sister's baby, and he'd tell

73

everyone the true story and get back at the Bradshaws that way.''

"Bill, this is fascinating. Barbara Bradshaw was terrified of Simon and hates him. She would be, if he was threatening to come out with something like that. And the other day when I was at the mill, Bradshaw and Simon were having a tremendous quarrel. What you're saying is, the Bradshaws had a very strong motive for shutting Simon's mouth.''

"Oh yes, Celia, that's right. But all those people in the pub are in it too, the ones that were shushing him to hold his noise and not come out with that bit of dirt.''

"Yes, you must tell me exactly who they were, let's go through the list. There was that death's-head butler of Colonel Templewood's, which seems very significant if Paul Templewood wasn't the child's father. Then we have Andrew Berridge, and Charley Englefield who's married to a Tunney, and Chris Wood who's married to a Berridge. Anyone else?''

"Perkins from the coal yard.''

"His wife's a Berridge. Who else?''

"The Tunneys, father and son. But Ron Tunney was just being the heavy policeman keeping things clean.''

"Nevertheless, they're all Tunney or Berridge connections.''

"There's two that weren't, Pat and Bob Pritchard. But they just took Simon out of the pub so I wouldn't bash him, they weren't in on the shushing.''

"Was Bradshaw there?'' Celia asked.

"No. I've not seen him in the Red Lion yet. Maybe he's not one for the pubs. Why d'you ask?''

"He's got the strongest motive for shutting Simon's mouth. But unless he was there in the pub, he wouldn't have known that you'd just quarrelled with Simon, and handed him a godsent opportunity to commit murder and shift the blame on to you.''

"If they're all in it together,'' Bill suggested, "one of the others could have tipped Bradshaw off that now would be a good moment to do it.''

74

"Quite true, and there's another thing that points to the Bradshaws. Simon was found half a mile downstream from the mill, so he must have been put in the water not very far below their weir."

"Oh yes, Celia, and what about this? Simon was drinking off his own money."

"Doesn't he usually?"

"No fear, he buys himself half a pint and cadges the rest. Then when he's flush like he was that night he stands his round. I reckon Bradshaw slipped him a quid or two to keep him sweet till he could knock him off."

"But he wasn't at all sweet, by the sound of it," Celia objected.

"He wouldn't be, if Bradshaw didn't give him enough."

"Bill, I could see Ted Bradshaw committing murder, but I don't think he's the sort to give in to blackmail. More likely Simon was spending what the Tidmarshes gave him to buy materials to put up their fence."

"That was weeks ago. He'd have spent it by now."

"Not if he made them give him far too much. They're very gullible."

"They're liars, I killed that goat a lot earlier than they told Ferris. You're just along the lane, you didn't hear the shot?"

"No. I'm sorry."

A long silence at the other end invited her to say she had, and confirm his alibi.

"I could tell Ferris I heard a big bang at half past ten," she volunteered. "But he wouldn't believe me, and it wouldn't take him long to find out that I spent that evening at a dinner party the other side of Welstead."

"Oh Celia, I made a packet of trouble with me bad temper. I'll never get out of this lot."

"Nonsense, Bill, things always look black in the small hours. Try to sleep, it'll feel quite different in the morning."

Sleep did not come to Celia at once. Lying awake, she decided on bold measures. There was no point in being furtive, sooner or later everyone in Melbury would know

75

that she was moving heaven and earth to avoid the inconvenience of having her head gardener whisked off to prison. She would take the bull by the horns and ask Ted Bradshaw whether he had an alibi for the time of the killing, and if he wanted to know why she was asking, she would tell him.

Next morning she rang him at his office at the mill. "There's something I need to talk to you about, preferably without Barbara. Can that be managed?"

"I should think so, she's going shopping in Guildford. Come round to the office about ten."

She arrived punctually, and stated her business at once. "You know the police have been questioning Bill Wilkins on suspicion of having killed Simon Berridge?"

"No," said Bradshaw. "I'm sorry to hear that."

"He didn't kill your brother-in-law, and I'm trying to find out who did."

"I see. But how can I help?"

"I want to eliminate as many people as possible, so I hope you won't mind if I ask you where you and Barbara were between ten and twelve that night."

He looked surprised. "Why us in particular? Are we part of a random sample, or have you picked on us for some special reason?"

"There is a reason, yes," Celia admitted. "You quarrelled rather violently with Simon the other day."

"Oh, yes, you saw that, didn't you? There was a very simple explanation. He asked me to give him a job at the mill, and told me I owed him one because he was Barbara's brother. I had to tell him I didn't employ drunks who'd never done a proper job of work in their lives, and he made some rather silly threats." Suddenly he was very cold and angry. "You're not suggesting, are you, that I took them seriously and killed him?"

"Let's say it's a possibility I'd like to eliminate."

"Do you seriously believe that we were terrified of what that pathetic drunken sot would do to us? So terrified that we killed him?"

"Not of what he'd do. The question is, what would he say?"

"What an extraordinary remark. Do explain."

"When Simon was in the pub that night, he was claiming that Paul Templewood wasn't the father of Barbara's baby, and threatening to tell everyone who was."

For a moment he was shocked into silence. "I'm disappointed in you, Celia. Do you really think that sort of maundering suggestion by a chronic drunk ought to be taken seriously?"

"A lot of people in the pub seemed to take it very seriously indeed."

"If they did, that's their affair. Simon thought up a bit of dirt to get his own back on us, and this village seems to have a hearty appetite for dirt. But what he chooses to say doesn't concern me, and where we were that night is no business of yours. What date did you say it was?"

She told him. He took out a pocket diary and turned over the pages.

"As it happens we were out till late that night, and if the police want to know where we were I shall tell them. But I'm not telling you, there's a limit to the amount of impertinence I'm prepared to put up with. And now good day to you."

Later that morning Detective-Inspector Ferris drove into the car park at Archerscroft in a far from friendly mood. When he asked Lewes CID to give him a run-down on the Anthea Clarkson affair, they had told him that a Mrs. Grant, Wilkins' employer, was a very clever woman and had played a significant part in solving that very complicated case. That was all very well, but Ferris had a low tolerance of amateur interference, especially if female. His promotion to Inspector was very recent, and he intended to do himself a bit of good career-wise by getting Wilkins convicted. Given half a chance, clever Mrs. Grant would do all she could to frustrate this plan and rescue Wilkins, who was undoubtedly her lover. She had already been trying to get the victim's widow to alter her story. How dare she interfere with his witnesses? He was not having that.

She received him from behind a neatly organised office desk, a fact which made him even more determined not to let this pretty little doll-like creature pull the wool over his eyes. "You saw Mrs. Berridge yesterday, I understand," he began.

"Yes."

"And you tried to persuade her to alter her evidence."

"I tried to persuade her to tell the truth. She's half mad, and I'm quite sure that nothing resembling a sexual assault ever took place. I think you should abandon your theory that Mr. Wilkins is a perverted rapist."

Ferris's worst forebodings were confirmed. He stood up and leant forward threateningly across the desk. "I'd watch my step if I were you, Mrs. Grant. I don't like people going round trying to influence my witnesses. If you know what's good for you, you'll keep away from Mrs. Berridge."

"I can hardly do that," Celia pointed out coldly. "She's employed here."

"Twisting her arm, are you? Threatening her with loss of employment if she won't withdraw her accusation and toe your line?"

"Don't be silly, you know the law as well as I do. She could take me to the cleaners for wrongful dismissal. You obviously intend to make Mr. Wilkins the victim of a miscarriage of justice, but I shall do everything possible to ensure that you don't succeed."

"You do that, Mrs. Grant, and I'll have you grovelling in court for trying to suborn witnesses and defeat the course of justice, so watch out and good morning to you."

The inquest on Simon Berridge produced a verdict of unlawful killing by a person or persons unknown. Bill and Celia thought it appropriate to display a total lack of interest in the proceedings, and did not attend. The funeral, which took place next day, was a different matter.

"It's awkward," said Celia, "but Joan's worked for us

for four years, we can't not go to her husband's funeral."

"Oh no, Celia. I'm not having them all pointing the finger at me and saying I killed him. You go, I shan't."

"If you stay away, they'll say it was because you're guilty."

"Let them. I don't give a damn what they think."

"Then you should. In a crisis like this, it matters a lot what the village thinks. Of course you must come."

"And have them shouting 'murderer' at me in front of the vicar and all?"

"There won't be a scene, the village doesn't behave like that. There'll be a tight-lipped silence and a few black looks, which we shall ignore. Go and put on a black tie and an innocent expression, and off we go."

In the forecourt of the crematorium, the mourners were standing around, waiting for the previous funeral to vacate the chapel. The Berridge and Tunney families were maintaining a tight guard of honour round Joan Berridge. When Bill and Celia arrived there were side-glances from people on the edge of the group, who looked away again at once. Evidently there had been a consensus decision that they should be ignored.

There was no such consensus about what should happen when two more or less estranged members of the family, Ted and Barbara Bradshaw, appeared. Each side was waiting to see how the other behaved. The Bradshaws advanced hesitantly across the tarmac, and Joan's guard of honour shuffled aside in some confusion to admit them. Barbara kissed her sister-in-law and Ted shook hands with her and tried to make conversation. But the response was chilly and the Bradshaws soon let themselves be frozen out. As they moved away the guard of honour closed in round Joan to exclude them.

Bill and Celia were being shunned by everyone till they were joined by Ann Hammond, who was there because she had employed Joan as her cleaning woman before she left to work at Archerscroft.

"Quite right to come and bring him," she whispered to Celia. "Did he do it?"

"No."

"Then tell him not to go around looking like a terminal case of indigestion, it gives the wrong impression."

Presently they were joined in their isolation by Jenny Foster, one of Celia's best workers, and fanatically loyal to her. Celia had seen her through a bad patch, with a baby due and a husband suddenly out of a job. Jenny was a cockney by birth, and usually treated the conspiratorial behaviour of the village as a huge joke.

"Look at them all," she said, tossing her head indignantly towards Joan's guard of honour. "Putting their heads together like American footballers to cook up more nastiness against Mr. Wilkins."

"They don't really believe Joan Berridge's nonsense, do they?" Celia asked.

"They'd make themselves believe the moon was made of black coffee if it suited them," said Jenny gloomily.

The funeral in front of them vacated the chapel by a side door, and the mourners began to file in. Jenny pulled Celia aside, and let Bill go on ahead with Ann Hammond. "I didn't want to say anything in front of Mr. Wilkins, but you need to watch that little runt of a policeman. He's dead keen to get Mr. Wilkins convicted, and he don't care how he does it."

In the chapel the Bradshaws made no attempt to claim a place with the family in the front pews, and the obsequies of the late but not universally lamented Simon Berridge began. The vicar, clutching at the only praiseworthy straw he could find in Simon's haystack of iniquities, remarked that they would all miss his "quirky sense of humour," then wisely devoted the rest of his homily to consoling the survivors. In due course the coffin sank through the chapel floor to the synthetic strains of solemnly canned music, and the mourners filed out through the side door into a cloister where the wreaths had been laid out for inspection and the widow was waiting to hold court.

Celia had solved the wreath problem by suppressing her own name and Bill's and sending an enormous one "from all at Archerscroft Nurseries." Getting Bill past Joan, weepy in black and flanked by grim-faced Tunney and Berridge relatives, was more difficult. She kissed Joan's moon face and gave her hand a squeeze, then made way for him. Joan put out a hand for him to shake, then withdrew it at the last moment in response to a stir of disapproval among her guardian kinsfolk. Bill choked down a murmur of protest and passed on.

"Did you see that, then?" he asked Celia as they walked back to the car park. "She don't believe I did it, she wanted to shake hands. They wouldn't let her. It's them, making her tell lies."

"Oh Bill, I know. But how do we prove it?"

As they turned into the car park, they saw the car. It was one of the big ones with "police" written all over it, painted to look noticeable. Ferris and a uniformed policeman were standing beside it.

Oh no, Celia thought, suddenly sick with apprehension. Not here, not now, with everyone watching and that huge car there, so that no one misses what's happening. Even Ferris wouldn't do that.

But she was wrong. Ferris advanced, dangling a pair of handcuffs, and spoke loudly enough for the whole funeral party to hear. "William Albert Wilkins, I have a warrant here for your arrest."

❧ FIVE ❧

"Fancy making a show of it, arresting him in front of everyone," said Jenny Foster indignantly as the police car drove away. "Who does Ferris think he is, a cop running riot in *Miami Vice*?"

She and Celia watched the police car disappear with Bill in the back, handcuffed to the uniformed policeman. He had protested against the handcuffs, but was told he was violent and had to be prevented from making another assault on the police.

"He can't arrest Bill," Celia stammered, still in shock. "He's got no real evidence."

"I'm sorry, Mrs. Grant, but don't you be too sure. He's been very busy, Ferris has."

Celia scarcely heard. It was Friday, she realised. "I must go after them and fix up about bail. Bill can't spend the weekend in a police cell with a lot of drunks."

But at the central police station in Welstead, she was told at the desk that there was no question of bail before the weekend. Moreover she could not see Bill, because of some regulation which she suspected Ferris of having invented.

"This is ridiculous," she protested. "Where's Inspector Ferris, let me talk to him."

Ferris made her wait for half an hour, then came out to

the desk looking foxily pleased with himself. "Thought you'd be round soon, Mrs. Grant," he said with a leer which implied that she was Bill's distraught mistress. "If it's bail you're on about, he'll be coming up in court on Monday, and you can apply for it then. But the police will oppose it."

"Really? Why?"

"Apart from the crime he's charged with, he has a record of violence. He assaulted a police officer and killed a farm animal with a firearm in pursuance of a dispute with a neighbour. There's also the matter of a violent sexual offence, which is still being investigated."

"You mean, you haven't decided yet whether to believe what that bat-witted woman is being made to say by her family? Congratulations on showing a glimmer of sense."

Ferris ignored this. "I'm opposing bail because he's a danger to the public. There's evidence from local people that he's always had an uncontrollable temper."

Evidence from which local people? Celia thought. The Berridges and the Tunneys, no doubt.

"Will he be allowed to have his toilet things and so on if I fetch them from his cottage?" she asked.

"That won't be necessary."

"Why not, for heaven's sake?"

He leered at her triumphantly. "Because we called there on our way here, to save you the trouble. In future you should choose your . . . friends more carefully, Mrs. Grant."

"Mr. Wilkins is my head gardener," said Celia coldly, "and there's no need to leer at me like that."

"I wasn't aware that I was leering," said Ferris, broadening the leer into an unpleasant grin. "I'm just amused that you know where to find your head gardener's toilet things."

The innuendo shocked Celia into loss of temper. "I suppose policemen are paid to have dirty minds," she hissed, "but you ought to be logical about it. If he's a perverted rapist with a hang-up about normal sex, he can't be my boy friend, can he?''

Ferris shrugged contemptuously and withdrew into the back premises of the police station, leaving Celia to rue her outburst. She knew perfectly well that tantrums in one so small and delicate-looking merely made her look ridiculous, why on earth had she not controlled herself?

Her next call was at her solicitor's. He was much too grand to concern himself with getting bail for a suspected killer, but arranged for a Mr. Stevens of the firm's litigation department to be in court on Monday and see what he could do. Then she headed for home to get organised, but was struck by a sudden thought as she reached the entrance to the Summerfield housing estate and drove in. Jenny Foster had said something at the crematorium, she had not paid proper attention—something about Ferris having unearthed some extra evidence. What? It seemed important to find out.

The Foster's house was on the opposite side to Joan Berridge's and further down the road. Jenny was in the kitchen giving the children their tea, and answered Celia's questions without ceasing to spoon scrambled egg into her youngest.

"Oh yes, Mrs. Grant, he's been in and out of the houses all down the road, like a ferret at the rabbit holes, Ferris is a good name for him. Putting on the charm like a door-to-door salesman, to get people to say Ooh yes, they saw Mr. Wilkins bashing Simon Berridge out in the road.''

"Oh dear, and what have they been telling him?''

"There's a few say they heard two people rowing out there late that night, but they didn't see who.''

"That's probably true," said Celia. "It looks as if some-one did attack Simon outside his house. But it wasn't Bill.''

"There's one lot besides Joan Berridge says it was him. The Perkinses at number twenty.''

"The man that works at the coal yard? His wife's a Berridge, that would explain it.''

"How they saw anything is a mystery because they don't

use their front room except for their son to take motorbikes to pieces in. They say they saw Simon running hell for leather down the road and Mr. Wilkins chasing after him. But they're the only ones as far as I know, apart from what Joan says.''

"You haven't been able to talk to her?''

"No fear, they give out that she's too upset to see anyone, but the family keep going in and out. Trying to make her stick to her story, I suppose. But she's that dippy, they probably have to remind her what it is.''

Celia thanked her and left, but arrived home in a fever of anxiety to be up and doing in defence of Bill. Surely there must be something she could get started on at once? Yes, of course. She would tackle the Tidmarshes about Bill's alibi.

They were extending their vegetable patch, breaking fresh ground with a furious energy which might more usefully have been devoted to removing rank weeds from the area already under disorderly cultivation. They had bought another goat, which they could well afford after making Celia pay through the nose for the one Bill had slaughtered. But this time they seemed to have taken proper advice, and the replacement was tethered with a stout chain to a solid-looking oak post.

"Ah, Mrs. Grant,'' said Tidmarsh, straightening his back. "Do come in and have a glass of Wendy's home-made mead.''

Evidently she was not in disfavour. Bill's delinquency had not rubbed off on her, probably because of the enormous compensation she had paid for the goat.

"I'm afraid this isn't a social visit,'' she explained. "I wanted to sort out a muddle which seems to have arisen about timings on the night when the goat was killed. Mr. Wilkins says it all happened at about half past ten, but I believe you told the police it wasn't till almost twelve.''

"Yes,'' said Tidmarsh firmly. "I'm sorry about the disagreement, but there's no doubt about the facts.''

"We were listening to a radio programme which ended

at ten to twelve," Wendy explained with a bold stare. "It had just finished when we heard Mr. Wilkins shoot poor Gertrude."

Celia was convinced that this was a fiction. In revenge for the killing of the goat they had lied maliciously. It had been killed around ten thirty, plunging the Tidmarshes into a state of indignant agitation in which they began composing the furious letter of complaint to Celia which they delivered first thing in the morning. By the time the broadcast started, they would have been in no mood to listen to the radio. She proposed to subject them to a detailed oral examination on what they claimed to have heard, and check their answers against a summary of the programme's gist which she would get from a contact who ran a gardening programme on the BBC.

"It must have been on a fascinating subject, to keep you up so late," she enquired.

"Indeed yes," said Tidmarsh. "It was all about the inordinate greed of commercial vegetable growers and the appalling risks they are prepared to take in the search for maximum profits."

"Really?" Celia murmured, convinced that the BBC could never have broadcast anything so loaded with invective.

"If food crops are grown by healthy, natural methods," he went on, "there is little or no damage by insects, or if it occurs it is limited to the appearance of the produce and does not affect the taste. But food grown under unhealthy conditions, cucumbers in greenhouses for instance, develops pests which have become resistant to the poisonous sprays which they have been using, so what do they do now? They pay research institutes to experiment with disease-producing viruses, and manipulate them by genetic engineering so that they attack insects which feed on unhealthily grown crops. These deformed viruses are then released into the environment to run amok. The possibilities are hair-raising."

"Oh dear," said Celia. "No wonder the BBC was worried."

"Needless to say, they played the danger down, the media are in the hands of the commercial growers' lobby. The scientists doing the research were allowed to say how safe it was, how carefully they'd tested the viruses for their genetic stability and their restricted spread in the environment. No one was allowed to challenge them, of course."

"Any day now," said Wendy, "they're going to start what they call 'controlled field tests in the environment,' but what if these horrifying perversions of nature escape from control and run wild?"

Were they making all this up? Celia wondered. If not, they must have heard part of the broadcast at least. "What sort of viruses were they talking about?" she asked.

"They're using a baculovirus called *Autographa californica*," said Tidmarsh glibly, "which is a registered insecticide in the United States, and modifying it with a genetic marker. They say they've replicated it through fifty generations to test for genetic stability, and done laboratory analyses of persistence on foliage and soil."

"And now they're testing it out of doors in what's supposed to be an enclosed ecosystem," said Wendy.

"The next step," Tidmarsh went on, "will be to muck about genetically with the original virus and produce what they call 'a set of custom-designed viral insecticides which will be specific and limited in their host range as well as limited in their ability to persist and have environmental impact'."

Celia was bewildered and suspicious. They had it off too pat, no one could have such total recall of a broadcast. But what was the explanation?

"You remember everything, almost word for word," she remarked.

"We taped it," said Wendy. "We often do when there's something of ecological importance. I typed some copies to give to friends. If you're interested we could lend you one."

"But perhaps you approve of interfering with nature?" Tidmarsh suggested.

"No, this sort of thing rather horrifies me," Celia told him.

"It doesn't horrify your friend Mr. Verney," said Wendy. "That institute where he works is up to its neck in this disgusting traffic in perverted genes."

"I'm sure you're wrong about that," said Celia. "They're concentrating on the use of insect predators to replace the sort of chemicals you object to."

The Tidmarshes greeted this with a knowing smile, to the effect that such wrong-headed ignorance about the facts of life was not worth arguing with, and renewed their offer of home-made mead. Celia refused, but had to let them lend her a typewritten transcript of the programme, which was a mass of underlinings, exclamation marks and sarcastic comments in the margin.

She was bewildered and alarmed. Had Bill really lied, to provide himself with a false alibi? As she walked home down the lane in a state of black depression, she stole another look at the Tidmarshes through their ragged hedge. They were laughing.

It was against her principles to drink alone. But her morale was so low that she decided to treat her despairing mood as an emergency and poured herself a whisky. On reflection, she refused to believe that Bill had lied about the time of the goat's demise. But the Tidmarshes must have heard the broadcast, there was no other explanation, unless . . . yes, it was a possibility. The BBC was thrifty in its scheduling, quite a lot of the evening's listening got a daytime repeat next day. She reached for the *Radio Times* and found that her hunch was right. They had missed the late night broadcast because they were too busy being indignant about the violent death of their goat. But they had remedied the omission by catching and taping the repeat on the afternoon of the following day.

Relieved by this discovery, she was enjoying her whisky when Peter Verney looked in to condole with her, having heard the news of Bill's arrest on his car radio while driving back from work. She spent some time bringing him up to date on recent developments, including her call on Ted Bradshaw.

"Interesting," Peter commented. "According to him the cupboard is devoid of skeletons, apart from any fictitious ones that Simon may have decided to furnish it with. Were you convinced?"

"I'm not sure. What he said was quite sound, but he blustered rather awkwardly when he said it."

"Alibi?"

"He says they've got one, but he wouldn't tell me what it was, except that he and Barbara were 'out' that evening."

"They could have got back from their dinner party or whatever in time to knock Simon off," Peter suggested. "Suppose they arrive home and find a very intoxicated Simon waiting on their doorstep, repeating his threats to tell all unless they come across with money. It would be the obvious thing for him to do after airing his grievance in the Red Lion. There's no one about, no one knows he's there. So the Bradshaws hit him on the head and dump him in the river."

"Well, he was put in the water somewhere below the weir at the mill, so you may be right. On the other hand, if they were out to dinner they wouldn't have known about Bill's quarrel with Simon. It was just a coincidence that they killed him at the best possible moment for getting away with it."

"Coincidences do happen, Celia."

"On second thoughts it may not have been one, there's another possible scenario. The Bradshaws aren't out to dinner. Someone who knows what happened at the Red Lion rings them and says, 'If you want to rid yourselves and us of an embarrassing nuisance, now's the moment to do it.' Bradshaw then ranges round the village in search of Simon and does the necessary. But why is it necessary? That's what I don't understand, and meanwhile this man Ferris is on a huge ego trip. He wants a conviction and he doesn't care how he gets it."

"I keep telling you, Celia, there's only one way to halt

his mad career. Find out what this earthy village secret consists of. If Paul Templewood wasn't responsible for Barbara Bradshaw's teenage predicament, who was? Find that out, and you're home.''

"That's all very well, but who's going to tell me? The Tunneys and the Berridges and Colonel Templewood's death's-head side-kick and the Bradshaws are all in it together, with their mouths firmly shut.''

"How about the rest of the population? If you ask around, you might find someone who isn't supposed to know, but does.''

"If we're going to be as crude as that, I might as well put up an advert card in the grocer's: 'Wanted, low-down about the true fatherhood of Barbara Bradshaw's illegitimate baby'.''

"We can narrow it down a bit. For instance, who was in the Red Lion that night apart from Tunneys and Berridges? There must have been someone unconnected with them who we can call on as a witness. Didn't Wilkins mention anybody?''

"No, and we can't get hold of him to ask him. Except—yes! There were two men who hustled Simon out of the pub to protect him from any more damage by Bill. Who did he say they were? I know, the Pritchard brothers, Bob and Pat. They're not connected with either family, nor are their wives.''

"Good,'' said Peter. "Why don't we drop in at the Red Lion at lunchtime tomorrow? They'll be there on a Saturday.''

Celia was about to agree enthusiastically, when it struck her that there might be a snag. She rummaged in her desk and fished out a neatly printed card, which confirmed her hunch. "They won't be there at lunchtime tomorrow, because Melbury's playing Little Barstow in the afternoon, and they'll both be in the team. You get pissed after cricket, not before.''

"How well-informed you are.''

"They send me their fixture list because I'm vice-president."

"Oh Celia. I'm impressed."

"Don't be. You get made a vice-president if you give them a five-pound subscription and take your turn on the rota for providing the teams with a gargantuan tea."

"Look, why don't we go down there and watch, and get the Pritchards into a corner while our side's batting?"

"Oh dear, what do I say to them?"

"You come straight out with it. You're trying to prove that Wilkins isn't guilty, and you'd like their account of what happened in the pub that night."

"My dear Peter, no. They wouldn't tell us anything, class solidarity. They'd clam up."

"What if they do? No harm will have been done. They'll tell the Tunneys and the Berridges that you're making enquiries, and that will put the fear of God into them."

Celia spent the next morning hard at work in the nursery. Saturday was always a busy day, with a crowd of customers in the frame yard. The part-time girls who manned the sales counter did not know enough to advise customers on their choice of plants or tell them how to look after what they had bought. She normally shared this chore with Bill, and his absence brought her near to tears as she told an eager young couple that what *Iris stylosa* "Mary Barnard" really liked was starvation conditions at the foot of a warm wall.

In due course Peter arrived to take her down to watch the cricket. She disliked the idea of leaving the customers to the tender but ignorant mercy of the Saturday girls. But time was passing, Bill was in a police cell. Any move to rescue him, however unlikely to yield results, would be better for her morale than doing nothing. So she let him drive her down to watch the peaceful spectacle of village cricket. Far away in the centre of the pitch, stately white-clad figures performed their slow-moving ballet on perfectly maintained grass, watched by spectators in deck chairs or on benches along the boundary.

As Celia and Peter looked for somewhere to sit, Colonel Templewood rose from his place on the verandah of the pavilion, and invited them to join him. This was a nuisance, it limited their freedom of action. But Colonel Templewood had paid for a new pavilion when its predecessor perished of wet rot, and the field itself was on his land. It was impossible to refuse an invitation to sit in the village's equivalent of the royal box.

The colonel was a crashing bore, as Celia knew to her cost. Being a widower, he was the last resort of hostesses desperate for a spare man. He had fallen to Celia's lot more than once at the grander county dinner-tables. His conversation was limited to long and pointless anecdotes on military and sporting subjects, all of which Celia had heard countless times. Despite his age he still had what his generation called "an eye for a pretty woman." In the intervals between his anecdotes he merely gazed at her and waited for her to be witty. I'm damned if I'm going to be witty now, she told herself as she sat down beside him. But fortunately there was no need. The colonel was totally absorbed in the game, and had an appropriate exclamation ready after almost every ball.

Melbury had won the toss. The Pritchard brothers, who were the village's star turn, were the opening pair. To Celia's annoyance they were hitting out lustily and looked set for a long partnership. Cricket bored her at the best of times, and with Bill in danger it fretted her intolerably. Why did the Pritchard brothers not get themselves caught or bowled or run each other out, so that she could question them?

Presently her patience was rewarded. Bob Pritchard lashed out at a ball that looked deceptively simple and was caught in the slips. As he started back towards the pavilion, Celia stirred in her deck chair, but Peter put a restraining hand on her arm. "Wait a bit. Ron Tunney and Andrew Berridge are in third and fourth wickets down."

"Why? What's the point?"

"If they're out of the way at the wicket they can't interfere."

It took almost an hour of desultory cricket to produce this state of affairs, with Tunney and Berridge otherwise occupied on the pitch, and the Pritchard brothers sitting on a bench in front of the pavilion with the rest of the team. Celia and Peter excused themselves to the colonel, and approached them. Peter's request to have a quiet word caused a general stir of interest, and on the next bench the colonel's manservant Burchett was agog. Mystified, the brothers followed Peter and Celia round to the side of the pavilion, where Celia explained that as Bill's employer she was concerned for him and felt it proper to make some enquiries. Could they tell her exactly what happened that night in the Red Lion?

This provoked an embarrassed reaction; they were being asked to pander to the obsessions of a silly middle-aged woman who doted ridiculously on her handsome but murderously violent young gardener. Their account of Bill's quarrel with Simon was halting and reluctant.

"And the quarrel started because Mr. Berridge accused him of raping his wife?" Celia asked.

More embarrassment. But they agreed that this was so.

"D'you think Mr. Berridge meant it? Or was it his idea of a joke?"

They looked at each other, then shrugged.

"Let's put it this way then. From the way he said it, did you believe Joan Berridge had been raped?"

The embarrassment became acute. "I dunno," said Bob unhappily.

"It's . . . not for us to say," Pat stammered.

"Anyway, you two marched Mr. Berridge out of the Red Lion."

"That's right. He'd had a few, and Wilkins would have half-killed him if he'd stayed."

"Very wise. Various people in the bar tried to stop him from going after Mr. Berridge, and when he did get out, Mr. Berridge was nowhere to be seen. What had you done with him?"

"There's an alley leads down beside the pub to where

the dustbins are. We hid him down there till Wilkins had gone."

"So you saw him go?"

"That's right. He looked around a bit, but it was dark down the alley and he didn't see us. Then he went off."

"And after that?"

"We went back in the bar."

"Taking Mr. Berridge with you?"

"No, he'd slumped down in the alley, all sleepy like. We reckoned someone ought to drive him home, so we went back in the bar to fix it. When we got back, he'd picked himself up and gone."

"So as far as you're concerned, he and Mr. Wilkins didn't meet again that night."

"That's right," said Pat.

Bob looked at him sharply. "Not outside the Red Lion, they didn't. What happened later, we can't answer for."

"Could I go back now to something that happened earlier? I believe Mr. Berridge was threatening to tell some scandalous story about the Bradshaws, because he had some grievance against them."

At once embarrassment gave way to shock. A barrier had come down. She was trespassing on forbidden ground.

"I never heard nothing of that," said Bob.

"Nor me neither," said Pat.

"Are you sure?" Celia persisted. "I've been told on good authority that he did say something of the kind."

"No, there was nothing like that said, you can ask anyone who was there." Bob was almost shouting in his anxiety to be believed. He looked round at the small crowd of spectators. "Hey, Charley. Here a moment."

Charley Englefield rose from his bench and joined them.

"Lady wants to know—what was it now?" said Pat.

Celia repeated her query. Englefield looked startled. "No," he replied promptly. "Simon was talking a lot of nonsense, but he never said nothing like that."

"And accusing Bill Wilkins of rape was part of the nonsense," said Celia, unable to resist the opportunity.

"Whether it's nonsense or not is a matter for the police," said Englefield severely.

"Fascinating," Peter commented when they had withdrawn. "The Pritchards, who aren't connected with the Tunneys or the Berridges, flatly deny that Simon threatened to reveal the frightful secret that causes such alarm. When they're driven into a corner they call on Charley Englefield for support. He's married to a Tunney and was one of the group that tried to shut him up when he spoke out of turn. In other words, the secret isn't a Tunney-Berridge monopoly, other people are involved in the conspiracy to protect it."

"Splendid," muttered Celia crossly. "Where does that get us? Nowhere. And we can't even prove that Simon said what Bill claims he said about Barbara's baby."

Peter looked grave. "That's true. If they lie to us about that, they'll lie about it to the dreadful Ferris."

"Lying is a thriving cottage industry in Melbury. This whole exercise was a waste of time, I'm going back to Archerscroft."

"Don't you think we should settle down again with Colonel Templewood?"

"Horrors, no. I'm off. Bill's been arrested. I've no time to be polite to a senile monomaniac with cricket on the brain."

"Don't you want to ask him who fathered the baby on Barbara if Paul didn't, and why Paul massacred half the village?"

"Now? While he's babbling about the butcher's batting average?"

"No, of course not. Make an appointment to go up to the house, but don't tell him what it's about."

I'm an idiot, Celia told herself, I should have thought of that. She sat down again beside Colonel Templewood, but found him so absorbed with the cricket that he did not surface into the real world in the pauses between the overs. Presently a wicket fell. The next man in had started out on to the pitch, fortified by the colonel's good wishes, and his returning predecessor was still too far away to be congratulated on his batting. She seized her opportunity. "Colonel, may I ask you something?"

He roused himself from his cricketing daze. "I'm sorry, I have been neglecting you. One gets so absorbed. What did you want to ask?"

"I've a problem I think you could help me to solve."

"Ah. Tell me, my dear."

"Not now, the cricket's too interesting. I was wondering if I could come up to the house some time soon to discuss it."

The colonel put on his eye-for-a-pretty-woman face. "Of course, my dear. Would you care to join me tomorrow for a very simple luncheon?"

Celia was horrified at the prospect of quizzing a bewildered and angry old gentleman about an eighteen-year-old tragedy over his Sunday roast, and pleaded a previous engagement. "But if I could drop in at about twelve on my way there—?"

"Of course, and you shall have a glass of my best madeira. Ah Harrison," he called as the butcher, fresh from his triumphs at the wicket, reached the pavilion. "Nearly got you behind the wicket, didn't they, in your second over. What happened?"

When this had been discussed to the colonel's satisfaction, Peter and Celia took their leave. She arrived back at Archerscroft in time to prevent a woman who gardened on chalk from buying six lime-hating Pernettyas and sold her six *Skimmia japonica fragrans* instead. Then she worked on till closing time, refused Peter's invitation to dine because of paperwork to catch up with, and spent a lonely evening plunged in gloom.

Next morning she dressed herself suitably for the non-existent lunch date she was supposed to be going to, and presented herself at Colonel Templewood's ancestral home, which Peter Verney had christened Nightmare Towers. It was a nineteenth-century Gothic pile in a state of grave neglect. Dark evergreen trees of sorts which the Victorians loved to excess loomed over long grass in what had once been the garden, and the curtains at the ground floor windows hung in filthy tatters, as if vampire bats had been attacking them. Celia always wondered why the colonel had let them get so dilapidated. Was drapery a female concern, overlooked since his wife's death? Or could new curtains not be afforded because he was still so bowed down by guilt for his son Paul's offence that he had impoverished himself in donations to the village?

Punctually at twelve she parked in the moss-grown drive. Her pull on the bell was answered by the death's-head Burchett, who received her with a mixture of butler-like formality and avid curiosity, and showed her into a book-lined study. She examined the room. A decanter and two glasses on a side table confirmed that she was expected. Despite his obsession with the cricket, the colonel had not forgotten. To judge from his shelves, his reading was confined to military subjects, including recent strategic studies as well as musty Victorian regimental histories. The silver cigarette box was a present from the officers of the First Battalion of the Border Regiment, but before she could read the inscriptions on the silver cups on the mantelpiece, the colonel joined her.

His first concern, as always, was to mention his close friendship with a distinguished soldier, now dead, who was a distant relative of Celia's. The two had become acquainted during the turmoil of the assault on the Normandy beaches in 1944 when the colonel, one of the youngest battalion commanders in the British army, had been among the first to lead his men on to the soil of continental Europe under fierce enemy fire. Celia's relative had commanded the flanking battalion, and the jokes they had exchanged as they ate corned beef in the shelter of a half-wrecked cinema formed one of the stock anecdotes which Celia had listened to at countless dinner-tables. He discharged it at her once more and poured her a glass of madeira, then said, "Now my dear Mrs. Grant, you wanted to consult me. What can I do for you?"

"It's about Simon Berridge. I expect you know that the police say his death wasn't accidental."

"So I hear. And now your head gardener, Wilkins, has been arrested."

"Yes. But I'm sure he isn't guilty."

The colonel's eyebrows shot up. "Really? Who else could it be?"

She explained: someone who wanted Berridge silenced had seized on his quarrel with Bill as an opportunity to commit murder and let Bill be suspected.

"But my dear Mrs. Grant, why should anyone want to 'silence' Berridge? He's a congenital liar, no one believes a word he says."

"That night in the Red Lion he was very drunk. He was threatening to blurt out some scandalous secret connected with his sister."

"His . . . sister? Ah yes, of course. He and Mrs. Bradshaw turn out to be brother and sister. But what could he possibly know to her discredit?"

"That was what I wanted to ask you, Colonel Templewood."

There was a long silence, and a marked cooling of the atmosphere.

"I'm sorry, I fail to understand you," he said in a carefully controlled voice.

"Lies are being told about this business. A group of village people are giving false evidence, trying to get Bill Wilkins convicted of a killing he didn't commit. They are men of the same age-group who've lived in Melbury all their lives. And they were all in their teens at the time of that tragic episode involving your son Paul."

The colonel was no longer a courteous old gentleman. She was being glared at by a very angry soldier. "How dare you drag that up? It's all over and done with, and has nothing to do with the matter we are discussing."

"I disagree. I'm sure Simon Berridge was threatening to tell the truth about that episode. I'm sorry, and I know this must be painful for you, but—he claimed that your son Paul

98

wasn't the father of Mrs. Bradshaw's baby.''

He was very red, and had begun to shout. ''This is an unforgivable impertinence, Mrs. Grant. Let me give you a word of warning. I am better informed about the affairs of the village than you may think. Your activities there are turning you into a figure of fun. A middle-aged woman who dotes publicly on a handsome young man is always ludicrous, but in your case the spectacle is also pathetic. Wilkins is obviously guilty. In a forlorn attempt to clear him, you go around inventing absurd conspiracies and accusing half the village of lying. People don't like that sort of thing, it causes offence.''

''I can't help that, I'm trying to prevent a miscarriage of justice.''

''Nonsense, you are deluded by your unhealthy passion for Wilkins.''

''I don't 'dote' on him,'' she retorted, furious. ''I've no more sexual interest in him than I have in that armchair. He's my head gardener and indispensable, I can't think how I'd carry on the business without him.'' Deciding that there was no point in being ladylike, she added, ''If your man Burchett got into trouble, wouldn't you try to get him out of it? Of course you would. And if I followed the dirty-minded reasoning you've just applied to me, I'd go round the village saying you were only doing it because he was your homosexual partner.''

For a moment she was afraid he was going to hit her, but he transformed the movement into an angry look at his wristwatch. ''I think you should leave to keep your luncheon appointment before you sink to even greater depths of vulgarity. And I advise you to stop speculating wildly about something that occurred long before you came to live in Melbury, and which still causes deep distress to the people who were involved.''

He rang the bell savagely. Burchett arrived to show her out, and eyed her with morbid inquisitiveness as he did so. As she drove away she wondered about his role in the guarding of the village secret. It was well known that he acted as the colonel's eyes and ears where village affairs were concerned. More than once, he had been suspected of prompting the colonel to reject appeals to his guilt-ridden charity which were obviously fraudulent. The colonel seemed to know a good deal about her activities, having no doubt got his information from Burchett. Why had Burchett been told to report in detail on matters concerned with Simon Berridge's death? Because Barbara's reappearance, and the threat of revelations from Simon which had resulted from it, gave the colonel cause for alarm?

Another thought. Was Burchett the go-between in a two-way traffic between the village and the colonel as they organised themselves in a joint campaign to protect a secret that all concerned were determined to keep?

❦ SIX ❦

Celia arrived early at the magistrates' court in Welstead to meet Roger Stevens, the man detailed by her solicitor to arrange bail for Bill. He proved to be blond, round-faced and disconcertingly young for the job, and seemed to believe that bad news was improved by being delivered in a bright, cheerful voice.

"I've seen Wilkins. He's in a very depressed state and he says he doesn't want bail," he announced with a happy smile.

"Oh what nonsense, why on earth not?"

"He says he doesn't want to have everyone in Melbury pointing at him and whispering. He'd rather be remanded in custody."

"How absurd. Let me talk to him."

Stevens beamed at her like the Cheshire cat. "I'm afraid you can't. Not now, he'll be up in court in a few minutes. Afterwards, perhaps. In any case, I doubt if we could get him bail in the teeth of police opposition."

"But how am I to run the nursery without him? Why shouldn't they give him bail?"

"He *is* charged with murder, Mrs. Grant."

"But that's absurd. The only evidence they've got is from a couple with a grudge against him, and a woman who's well known to be only half there. Anyway, why murder? If you hit someone too hard and kill them without meaning to, it's manslaughter.''

His smile took on overtones of pity. "Not if you throw the body in the river afterwards, unfortunately.''

A few minutes later William Albert Wilkins was up in court amid tasteful light oak panelling, being charged with the murder of Simon Francis Berridge. He was unshaven and scruffy-looking, and was scowling as if, Celia thought, he wanted to be mistaken for the sort of violent criminal who should not be given bail. As he had not applied for it he was remanded in custody for a month and escorted out of the dock.

"If you'd like a word with him now, Mrs. Grant," said Stevens, "I can probably arrange it for you.''

She followed him out of the courtroom and down into the basement of the building. An iron grille blocked off the entrance to a carbolic-smelling passage lined with depressingly chipped white tiles. Bill was sitting with another prisoner on a bench halfway along it. Stevens exchanged a few words with the policeman on duty, who opened the gate and let them through.

Bill looked up at her from the bench without enthusiasm. "Hello, Celia.''

"Hello, Bill, we'll have you out of here in no time. I've several promising leads already.''

He shrugged, as if to say that such talk, though well meant, did not deceive him.

"Don't look at me like that, Bill. It's true. Someone killed Simon because he threatened to open up the Barbara Berridge can of worms.''

"That bastard Ferris says Simon never said nothing about that. He's asked Ron Tunney and the others, they say they never heard it.''

"Then they're lying, aren't they?''

"Everyone's lying, Celia. I'll never get out of this fix.''

"Nonsense, we've cracked tougher nuts than this.''

"There's no nut tougher than them nasty village people

when they get in a corner to hush up something dodgy. It's like one of these Chinese secret societies you read about in books."

He was right about that, Celia thought despairingly, and too intelligent to be consoled with empty words of hope. "Anyway, I'll do my best. Why didn't you want bail?"

He shrugged the question off. "Celia, even if I get off, I'll not be coming back to Melbury. Not ever."

"Oh no, Bill, why?"

"If they let me off, it'll be because they can't prove I'm guilty—it's called 'the benefit of the doubt.' They'll never find out who really done it, how could they? And if I was to go back to Melbury when it's over, they'd all say, 'He was lucky, he did it but he got off.' I'm not staying there to face that, with them all pointing the finger at me."

Celia was near to tears. "Bill, are you sick of working with me, d'you want to leave Archerscroft?"

"Oh no, Celia, but I got to."

"No, you haven't," she said, and decided suddenly on shock treatment. "Don't be such a damn wimp, have a bit of confidence in me, do. Of course I'll find out who did it and get you cleared. When I've collected all the evidence I shall serve it up to Mr. Stevens here and he'll go into action. And meanwhile there's no reason why you should sit on your bottom in your cell twiddling your thumbs. To start with, I shall bring you the autumn catalogue, and you can proof-read it for me."

While they talked, the bench on either side of him had filled up as other prisoners were brought down from the court. Presently two policemen arrived and marshalled them all into single file, ready to be led away to the police van. When Bill's turn came to move off, he said, "Bye, Celia," and walked away without looking back.

Celia turned to Stevens. "Which prison will they take him to?"

He corrected her cheerfully. "He'd be lucky, prison's a privilege nowadays. You don't get to one straight off, all the remand prisons are full. It'll be a police cell for him, shared with one other if he's lucky, two if he's not." He looked at his watch. "Well, that's that for the moment. The committal proceedings won't be for another month. We'll meet again when we know the exact date."

"Good. I'll try to have the evidence that he didn't do it ready by then."

"Actually, there's no hurry. At the committal proceedings the prosecution has to prove that there's a case to answer, that's all that happens. The defence evidence isn't produced till the actual trial in six or nine months' time."

"Horrors, you mean Bill rots in a police cell till then?"

"Oh, they'll probably find room for him in a prison in due course."

"What happens if I get cast-iron proof within the next month that someone else did it?"

His bright smile vanished. "Instances have been known where the defence produced evidence at the committal stage that there was no case to answer. But it's very rare."

He was keeping his thoughts to himself, but she could guess what they were: Mrs. Grant has been a client of ours for years, but she is making a fool of herself over a man young enough to be her son, who is of course guilty because no innocent man would have behaved as he did just now. There is going to be a fiasco, and if the firm loses a valued client in the process, I shall be blamed for handling the thing badly. . . .

"I'll be in touch, then," she said and left him.

Her next call was at the offices of the local paper to consult its back files. She had spent part of the previous afternoon wandering round the churchyard at Melbury and studying the tombstones, in particular those of David Black and four teenagers, Albert Wood, James Englefield, Richard Berridge and William Gurney. Other details of the inscriptions suggested that Albert Wood had been the postman's brother, Richard Berridge one of the garage Berridges, and James Englefield a brother or cousin of the village shop. There were some Gurneys who were agricultural labourers, but as far as she knew, there was no family called Black living in the village. The interesting point was that according to their tombstones all five had died on the same day, 28th October 1960. Having thus discovered the date of Paul Templewood's massacre without exposing herself to more ridicule by asking anyone, she knew exactly which back numbers of the paper to ask for, and was soon studying a yellowing front page story headed *Landowner's son in tragic shooting affair*.

It was an account of the inquest, and it explained something which had always puzzled her: how had a teenage boy with a shotgun managed to kill five people and wound several more, presumably reloading at intervals, before someone overpowered him? There was an unexpected explanation. The massacre had not happened while the shoot was in progress, but during the lunch break at the Red Lion, where the guns and beaters were gathering for beer and sandwiches at the colonel's expense. The beaters, men from the village and their teenage sons, had foregathered in the yard behind the pub, waiting for the colonel to arrive. When he did, Paul Templewood was with him. But instead of following his father into the bar, he rounded on David Black the butcher and young Richard Berridge, who was standing beside him. He shot them at point blank range, and dashed out of the yard.

In the confusion and concern for the dying pair, no one wondered at first where Paul had gone. Two beaters ran round to the front of the Red Lion and looked up and down the road without seeing him. Meanwhile two more shots were fired, killing William Gurney and James Englefield. No one knew where they were coming from or where to take shelter, and some time passed before it became clear where Paul was. He had barricaded himself into the pub's outside WC, and was shooting through a small window, more like a ventilation hole, which he could reach by standing on the seat. Its field of fire covered the only exit from the yard. Before the panicked crowd could escape into the pub through the back door, Albert Wood had been shot dead, and two other boys, who were too far away to be killed by gunshot, had been wounded: Simon Berridge, who lost an eye, and Pat Pritchard.

Attempts were made to persuade Paul to come out and give himself up. The police arrived in force and tried to parley with him through the door of his cubicle, but he drove them back by shooting at their legs through the gap under the door. Colonel Templewood, flat against the outside wall of the lavatory, talked to his son to no effect, but refused to tell the coroner what he had said. The assumption was that he had told Paul there was only one honourable way out after what he had done. But there was an agonised wait for over four hours before Paul summoned up enough courage to shoot himself.

Celia approved of the coroner, who had asked all the right questions. Had Paul been in the Red Lion before, could he have familiarised himself with the layout? In other words, did he know in advance about the lavatory window and its field of fire, in which case the shooting was perhaps premeditated? The landlord rejected with horror the suggestion that he would allow anyone under age to enter his premises. Paul must have gone in there to shoot himself, discovered the window and decided that he might as well take one or two others with him. Was there any enmity between him and David Black, the only adult victim? None, according to the widow, as far as she knew they had had no dealings with each other. Had Black said anything to Paul which might have annoyed him and prompted him to shoot? Various people thought that Black had passed some remark, but they had been too far away to hear what it was.

How about Paul's state of mind earlier in the day? He seemed very depressed and nervous, Colonel Templewood said, and his shooting was very erratic. When had his disturbed state first become apparent? The colonel had initially noticed it during the summer holidays, and he was much worse when he came home from his boarding school for half term, just in time for the shoot. Asked if he knew the reasons behind his son's depression, he said that at first he had attributed it to Paul's doing rather badly at school, where he was below average academically and not much good at games. He added that other very distressing matters had since come to light which offered a different explanation of Paul's state of mind. He understood that they would be touched on in the police evidence.

Before this evidence was produced, a surprise witness was called, fifteen-year-old Barbara Berridge. She was in tears and had to be allowed to sit down in the witness box. She was pregnant, she said, and Paul Templewood was the father.

The coroner did not take this at its face value without further enquiry. Where had the couple met? At an evening barbecue organised in aid of church funds. And after that? In barns and under hedges on his father's land. "It was July and very hot weather," she explained, "and he was unhappy and I was sorry for him and one thing led to another." Asked why Paul was unhappy she replied, "I don't know, he just was." Some of the things he had said frightened her. She had wanted to break with him, but was afraid of what he might do if she did. Had he ever threatened to kill anyone? Yes. Himself.

Up to this point it was possible to take a sympathetic view of the wretched Barbara as an innocent village maiden betrayed by the squire's half-mad son under the lust-enhancing influence of a heat wave. But the police evidence put her in a rather different light. According to them, Paul had been desperate for money throughout the late summer and autumn, and had been none too particular about how he got it. In late August and early September small valuables, silver and china ornaments and the like, had started to vanish from houses in the neighbourhood belonging to friends of the Templewoods and were later offered for sale at secondhand shops in nearby towns by a youth who corresponded with Paul's description. There had been trouble at his expensive boarding school too. Money, watches and other saleable things such as cameras had been stolen from boys' lockers, and although the culprit had not been positively identified Paul was under strong suspicion. Back at

107

home for half term, he had been caught shoplifting at a camera shop in Guildford on the day before the shoot, and was due to appear in court on the following Monday.

The wretched Barbara was recalled to the witness box and asked if she had demanded or received money from Paul. Sobbing and angry, she had denied ever receiving a penny from him. Despite a lot of pressure from the coroner, she persisted in her denial. But although no one put it into words, the implication was clear. Barbara Berridge was blackmailing the squire's son by threatening to tell his parents. And Paul, terrified of his stern martinet of a father, was scraping up money to buy her silence. The shoplifting charge was the final blow which had pushed him over the edge. Barbara was morally responsible for a tragedy which had killed five people and wounded two more.

So that was the official version, Celia thought as she drove back to Melbury. It was quite bad enough to make a teenage girl, in disgrace and uncertain of herself, want to get out of the place and never come back. There might well be another version, even worse, but what could it consist of? Rather than waste time speculating, she headed for the High Street instead of going back to Archerscroft. According to Ann Hammond, her doctor husband had always said there was something odd about the shooting tragedy which puzzled him. She would ask him what it was.

Jack Hammond was out, but Ann was at home in the elegant Georgian house halfway down the street, and Celia put the query to her. Ann treated her to a long, searching stare. "He'll be back for lunch, I'll ask him. But look here, Celia, you need to be careful. Jack and I are getting a lot of feedback from the village, through the surgery and the cleaning women and so on. You're asking questions. They don't like it, the way you're stirring up all this stale old mud."

"I'm sure they don't, but the answer I'm looking for is down there in the mud. When I make a few casual enquiries, alarm bells start ringing all over the village and Colonel

Templewood tells me severely not to meddle in things that are not my concern.''

"Celia, you didn't ask *him*! Did he burst into tears?"

"No, I was ticked off in a parade-ground bellow."

"Well, there you are, he's touchy about it. I say, is your handsome Wilkins innocent?"

"Yes."

"You're sure?"

"Absolutely."

"Not kinky? No fixation for obesity? No fun and games with fat Joan Berridge?"

"Certainly not, he'd rather die."

Ann nodded. "I can believe that, Joan made it up. She's such a fool, she could have seen the other sort of rape growing somewhere, the yellow sort they have in fields, and it unsettled her and she got mixed up. What can you expect, though, her mother was quite barmy. But Celia, what about the other bit, the killing? What I mean is, I see how it could have happened. Joan says 'rape', Simon says 'rape' and Wilkins hits him a bit too hard. Silly of him to dump the mortal remains in the river, but no jury would treat it as murder. If he owned up now I'm sure he'd get quite a light sentence."

Celia controlled her voice carefully. "I'm sure you mean well, Ann, but I can't afford to think what you're thinking, and I'm determined not to. Do remember to ask Jack, won't you, what it was that worried him about the shooting incident."

"Very well, Celia. But I warn you, you're barking up the wrong tree."

Celia drove back to Archerscroft, to find a letter waiting for her from Joan Berridge. She was going away for a time, to recover from the shock. She did not know when she would be back. She did not want to return to her job at Archerscroft after what had happened.

"She went off Saturday," said Jenny Foster when Celia went to consult her about this in the frame yard. "George and Kathleen Tunney came and took her in their car. She'll be tucked away somewhere with relations, under guard. They're afraid you'll get at her and make her change what she thinks of as her mind.''

Was that the explanation, or was there an innocent one? It was natural for a woman to want a change of air after losing her husband, and Joan might well feel that she had fouled up her relations with Celia and made herself unwelcome at Archerscroft. Celia looked at the letter again. It was Joan's writing, but the punctuation and grammar were better than usual and there were fewer spelling mistakes. Had it been written under dictation? Possibly, but how could one be sure?

At lunchtime Ann telephoned. ''Jack says he's sorry, but he can't help you. Medical etiquette. Confidentiality of the doctor-patient relationship and all that.''

''But it all happened eighteen years ago. Were they his patients? Anyway, most of them are dead.''

''Not all of them. Sorry, Celia.''

Of course, Celia thought. One of Jack Hammond's patients was still very much alive. Barbara Berridge and family had consulted him all those years ago about her pregnancy. What was confidential about it? Obviously, that Paul was not the real father. As she suspected, the painful scene at the inquest was a cover-up for something even worse.

Assume that the father was a teenager living in the village. The boy's family are distraught. So are George and Kathleen Tunney, the uncle and aunt who have brought up orphaned Barbara. Then the disaster at the Red Lion happens. Paul Templewood is dead. Someone has a brilliant idea. Barbara is to say that Paul was the child's father. He is not there to deny it. The boy who is really responsible gets off scot-free. George and Kathleen Tunney reckon that Colonel Templewood can be made to stump up handsomely. A teenage girl wandering round the village in a hugely swollen state is no advertisement for the way her uncle and aunt brought her up, perhaps the colonel will pay up enough for this embarrassing sight to be removed elsewhere.

Then comes the inquest. It will be an ordeal for Barbara,

but it is in everyone's interest, including hers, for her to tell a lie. She is only fifteen, she is in disgrace and both the families involved are bullying her, so she does what she is told. What nobody knows till she has given her evidence and stood down, is that the next witness will be a policeman telling the court that Paul had been stealing to raise money, with the implication that the money was for her. The Tunneys and the boy's family have led her into a trap, the whole village is holding her responsible for driving Paul over the edge and causing the disaster at the Red Lion. No wonder she refuses to return to Melbury after she has had the child.

No sooner had Celia reached this conclusion than doubt set in. A teenage pregnancy was something most villages took in their stride; there had been several since she came to live in Melbury and no one had treated the culprits as lepers. What was different in Barbara's case, why was it necessary to tell a thundering lie? No doubt the colonel's money would come in useful, but was it worth the risk? Something might have turned up in evidence at the inquest to throw doubt on her claim that Paul was the child's father, or even disprove it. And if the awesome secret was only about a baby being blamed on the wrong father eighteen years ago, why were the colonel and the village making such a carry-on about it? This whole line of reasoning was mistaken, she decided. It was not to protect Barbara that the Hammonds had hidden behind medical etiquette. They had used it as an excuse to avoid getting involved, because a doctor could not afford to take sides in village politics.

She was utterly bewildered and miserable, but work at Archerscroft had to go on, and there were Bill's jobs to be attended to as well as her own. While she was away in Welstead she had left Jenny Foster in charge, as the most sensible person available. "You better have a look at those little cyclamen, Mrs. Grant," she said when reporting on the morning's events, "the ones in the big glasshouse. They look a bit moth-eaten to me."

Celia was horrified. The next batch of *Ambliseius*, which ought to have been introduced to their prey three days ago, lay in her desk drawer, forgotten in her worry about Bill. She fetched the box and went down to the glasshouse. Jenny had not exaggerated. The proportion of corms with roughened, wrinkled leaves had increased dramatically, while others showed signs of stunted growth. Some of them were so badly infested that she wanted to throw them out, but would she be throwing out the predators as well as the pests? She opened the box and spread the flour and insect mixture as evenly as she could, then phoned Peter at work. He promised to look in on his way home and advise on what to do next.

He came and looked. "I'm afraid it's got out of control, I don't think the *Ambliseius* are going to deal with it effectively. We'll try something else. A spray."

"But didn't you say sprays weren't effective against it?"

"This is a fungus that you apply in solution with water, I'll give you the proportions. You have to keep the humidity high for a day or two afterwards, and it's probably toxic to *Encarsia* and *Phytoseiulus*, but you can reintroduce them later."

"Oh Peter, I'm afraid this is my fault. I forgot to put that last batch in because I was so worried about Bill."

He thought for a moment. "Celia, I want to talk to you about Bill. Come home and we'll do it over a drink."

Oh, not again, Celia thought. She did not welcome the prospect of yet another lecture about not making a fool of herself in the eyes of the village, but there was no help for it. They set off down the lane, and Peter kept up a barrier of small-talk till they reached his house, an Elizabethan cottage of the horrider sort, with low ceilings and beams in awkward places and doors that let in draughts. There were also a good many cobwebs, and she settled down to contemplate the inadequacies of his cleaning woman while listening meekly to the threatened lecture.

"Celia, I've been meaning to tell you this for some time," he began. "I'm sure there's an innocent explanation, that's why I haven't worried you with it before, but I think you ought to know."

112

"Goodness. I hope this is going to be less alarming than it sounds."

"There's a problem, I'm sorry to say, about the time of the goat-shooting incident. The Tidmarshes said it happened shortly before midnight, and you decided they must be lying. I'm afraid they weren't."

"Really? Who says?"

"I do, very reluctantly. You see, I'd been working late that night at the lab, and on the way home I overtook Bill walking up the lane. If he says he was back at Archerscroft shooting a goat by half past ten, he's wrong. It was much later than that."

"Peter, it's terribly easy to make a mistake about times."

"I wish I could say I had, but it's out of the question. I was doing something with a centrifuge that needed accurate timing, so I was watching the clock. I switched the thing off at eleven twenty. Allow ten minutes for clearing up and getting down to the car park. I must have left the lab at about half past eleven and even at that time of night with the roads clear the journey takes all of fifteen minutes. So it must have been at least a quarter to twelve when I overtook Bill walking up the lane."

Celia was shattered. "But Peter, you're saying he hasn't got an alibi. He'd have had all the time in the world to kill Simon and dump him in the river."

"I know. I feel an absolute heel, having to bring this up. But facts are facts and science, unlike justice, cannot be blind."

"Why didn't you tell me before?" she asked, choking back tears.

"I didn't realise at first that the timing was significant, not till you told me about your attempt to trip the Tidmarshes up about that radio programme you thought they hadn't heard. When I did realise, I couldn't bring myself to say anything because I knew it would upset you horribly."

"Have you told the police?"

"Good Lord no, what d'you take me for? I haven't and I shan't. As I say, I'm sure there's an innocent explanation."

113

He doesn't believe that, she thought. He's saying it to soften the blow. Bill didn't confide in me, there's no innocent explanation of that. She jumped up nervously from her chair and said, "I must go home."

"Oh no you don't, Celia, I'm not letting you spend the evening alone over there, having the glooms about this."

"I shall have frightful glooms about it wherever I am."

"Very well, but here's what we'll do. I shall cook us some bacon and eggs, and when we've eaten it we'll cast care aside at the cinema in Welstead, they've got a Woody Allen film on. And you can have your glooms tomorrow."

Too shocked to object, she let him have his way, but could only pick at the bacon and eggs.

"Never mind," he said. "Some people overeat hugely under stress, and they say the government gives huge official lunches for no one in particular when there's a crisis. You react the other way, but I wasn't to know."

The film was a meaningless jumble of images and words, her mind was blocked off from taking it in. It was also blocked off from taking in what Peter had told her, except as a dull ache of misery, dominated by the memory of Bill sitting in deep depression in the corridor at the magistrates' court, convinced that he would be found guilty and that nothing could be done about it. What conclusions could be drawn from that? None, in her present state of mind. When she tried to puzzle it out, her thought processes went numb.

The mental paralysis lasted through the night and into the next day, gradually transforming itself into a guilty feeling that she ought to be doing something. But what? Colonel Templewood, the Bradshaws, the Hammonds and the village in general had erected a wall of silence round the Red Lion tragedy. Was there a dark secret? How could she possibly find out? And if she did, was it relevant? She would have to visit Bill soon in his cell at Welstead police station, but could not decide what to say to him and put it off. So she worked on at Archerscroft in a daze of worry, doing the most urgent of Bill's jobs as well as catching up on neglected ones of her own.

After another day of drugging herself with work in the nursery, she nerved herself to get permission and visit him. When he was let out of his cell into the corridor to talk to her, she was shocked. His face was thin and drawn and there were dark circles under his eyes. They were three to a cell, he told her, locked in for twenty-three hours a day.

"They say it's better when you been found guilty," he told her.

"Not when, *if*," she corrected.

"Oh Celia, I been found guilty by the village already. It don't matter what the judge decides."

"What nonsense. It's the only thing that matters."

He looked at her doubtfully. "That solicitor of yours came yesterday. He says nothing's decided when I come up in court again next month. The police have to say why they want me tried, that's all. Then I go back in the cell and wait for months till the case comes up. I can't stand it, shut up for months in that cell with them two men. One of them's gay. Tried it on with me. I had to hit him."

"Bill, you really must try to stay calm when people make a pass at you. Women have to do it all the time."

"But there was this other feller there, staring at us. Filthy, it was."

"Did you do much damage?"

"Only a front tooth and a cut lip."

"Oh dear, being violent while you're on remand won't help you at your trial."

"I'll not wait to be tried. I made up me mind."

"Bill! What on earth d'you mean?"

"When I'm up in court again I'll say I did it. I'll say I never meant to hit Berridge so hard, and when he was dead I lost me head and put him in the river. Stevens says if I say that, I'll get tried quick, and go down for two or three years, and it'll be over with."

"But Bill, how am I to manage without you for all that time?"

"I've told you, Celia," he said wearily. "I can't come back to Melbury. Not ever."

"Not even if you're in the clear because I've found out who killed Simon?"

"Oh very funny, however would you do that?"

"I've no idea, but I shall do my damnest. Bill, I've got to ask you this, are you quite sure you've told me everything?"

"Course I have. We been through it again and again."

"What I mean is, you couldn't possibly be mistaken about the time you got back to Archerscroft and shot the goat?"

"What d'you mean, mistaken?" Suddenly he was very angry. "Course I'm not mistaken. That's not what you meant though, is it? You was saying, did I tell a lie about the time, and will I tell you the truth now?"

"No, Bill, I—"

"Yes you did. I smelt a rat soon as you come in, you was looking different somehow. You think I killed Berridge, don't you?"

"No, it's just that—"

"Yes you do, you're being dodgy with me," he shouted, scarlet with anger. "Oh Celia, I never thought it of you." He stood up to end the interview. "Don't come back here, I'd rather not. And I don't want to see that Mr. Stevens of yours no more."

"Bill, come back!" she shouted as he walked away. He halted for a moment, then went on his way without turning to look.

Celia drove back to Melbury, thinking hard but terrified of the conclusions she might reach. What had Bill been trying to convey? He intended to plead guilty. Why? Because he was guilty? If so, why had he bothered to pretend to her that he was innocent? Was he innocent, and was his anger genuine when he suspected her of doubting it? Or was he guilty, and was the savage parade of anger intended to make sure she felt as miserable as he did? That would be unlike the Bill she knew, but how could one tell how even one's closest friends would behave in this sort of crisis?

Back at home, she settled down in an armchair for a good

weep, but had scarcely begun when Peter Verney arrived and offered to take her out to dinner.

"It's kind of you, but no thanks," she told him. "I must finish the VAT returns tonight."

"You're not in a fit state to work this evening. You've been crying."

"I daresay, but I'm quite capable of weeping on my own shoulder, and the VAT returns should have been in last week."

"Went to see Bill Wilkins, did you?"

She nodded, and was grateful when he refrained tactfully from asking what Bill had told her.

"Look, Celia, you mustn't kill yourself doing two people's jobs while Bill's away. Can't I help? I've got the right scientific background and I'm handy with plants."

"Thanks a lot, but Jenny Foster's a very sound plantswoman, she's doing a lot of Bill's jobs for me. I'm only overworking to stop myself thinking."

"I know, this is beastly for you. But do let me know if there's anything I can do. Talking of which, I really called to give you this."

He handed her a pharmaceutical phial. She stared at it, knowing what it was.

"The fungoid spray," he reminded her. "For your cyclamen mites."

She took the bottle. "One of the *Verticilliums,* is it? Like the stuff commercial firms use for whitefly on cucumbers?"

"That sort of thing. But it's specific for *Tarsonemus pallidus,* alias the cyclamen mite. The instructions are on the bottle."

She thanked him and dismissed him without offering a drink, using the VAT returns as her excuse. They were indeed late, and she forced herself to concentrate on them for most of the evening, nibbling oddments from the refrigerator from time to time. When the returns were finished and out of the way she was attacked by a guilty feeling that she ought to be doing something, no matter what, by way of investigation. There was one angle that had occurred to

117

her as just worth looking into, though it was probably marginal and off the point. But the telephone was beside her and it was not indecently late. She rang her uncle Hugo, a retired ambassador of great distinction who lived on the other side of Lewes and knew everything there was to know about the grander inhabitants of Sussex.

"Uncle Hugo? D'you remember that dinner we were at last winter at the Framlinghams'? I want to ask you about something you said."

"Dear me. Which of my senile burblings are you going to quote in evidence against me?"

"Actually, it was something you didn't say. I'd copped Colonel Templewood at dinner as usual, and when you and I got together afterwards over coffee I said wasn't it odd that such a brave soldier had to be such a crashing bore, and did being brave demand so much mental effort that there was no room in his mind for anything else? And you gave me a look and said, 'H'm.' I asked you what 'H'm' meant but you wouldn't tell me. Would you mind awfully telling me now?"

"I'd rather not. This is one of those unhappy stories that one only dishes out on a need-to-know basis."

"But I do need to know," said Celia, and explained why.

"Oh dear, you seem to spend your time nowadays brewing up nasty kettles of fish. Why that nursery garden of yours doesn't go bankrupt, I can't imagine."

"Nor can I, but tell me about Colonel Templewood."

"Well, you remember Ian Stuart-Kennedy, that cousin of mine and your mother's who left Glendurgan to the Edinburgh Stuart-Kennedys?"

"Indeed I do. The first time I got landed with the colonel he started on an unbelievably long and boring story about how he'd crawled up hill and down dale on his belly in that part of the Highlands, in pursuit of some stag. In desperation I interrupted to say that I'd stayed at Glendurgan as a child, and it stopped the flow marvellously. The name rang a bell with him because it turned out that he was a wartime buddy of Cousin Ian's, and now I get the same not very funny story about Cousin Ian every time, usually between the starter and the main course.''

"H'm. He wouldn't have been so keen to claim acquaintance if poor Ian had still been alive. I got this story from Ian, and I have every reason to believe it's true, but it's not very nice and you must promise not to repeat it to anyone unless you absolutely must.''

"Very well, I promise.''

"You see, there were three battalions brigaded together for Overlord to go in with the first wave at Arromanches, a battalion of the Border Regiment commanded by Templewood, some Seaforths commanded by Ian and something else Scottish, I don't remember what. Templewood was one of the youngest and also the most promising battalion commanders around. He was a first class leader of men, his training exercises were thoroughly imaginative, everyone thought the world of him, including his own junior officers and men. That was during the training period though, he'd never been in action. When it came to the point on D-day, getting out of the landing craft and fighting his way up an exposed beach under heavy fire proved altogether too much for him, he couldn't cope. His men performed marvellously, because he'd trained them well. But he just sat in his battalion headquarters in a state of nervous collapse, too terrified to give orders even. The brigade major had to take over from him and he was sent home.''

"In disgrace?'' Celia asked.

"I suppose so, but there was one bit of soldiering that he was brilliant at, and the army very sensibly didn't waste it. He spent the rest of his military career, during and after the war, training recruits.''

"Oh dear. This story he tells is about what an enjoyable party D-day was and how he and Cousin Ian sat in this ruined cinema eating bully beef and laughing their heads off about it all. And he gives the village to understand that he's a terrific war hero. Oh dear, how appallingly sad.''

"Yes. It's rather pathetic really. Don't tell anyone, will you?''

119

Interesting, Celia thought. The snakelike Burchett was the colonel's army batman. Does he know this story, and if so how does it affect the relationship between the two? That night she lay awake a long time thinking, then suffered her standard nightmare, to the effect that she was a saxifrage and potbound. She kept shouting for Bill to come to her rescue but in vain, he was drinking in the Red Lion and took no notice. Next morning she felt completely exhausted, but busied herself at the nursery, turning on the misters over the cyclamen to bump up the humidity, then spraying on the fungus mixture. Then she potted on a batch of double primroses, an Archerscroft speciality, which had been divided in the spring.

Two more days passed. She felt she ought to be up and doing on the detection front but could think of nothing to detect. The fungus spray seemed to be having an impact on the cyclamen, and she told Peter so when he looked in on his way home to enquire.

"I'm glad," he said. "I wish your other troubles could be solved as simply."

His hand was on the back of her chair, and he let it fall on to her neck and shoulder. Embarrassed, she made a slight movement which he interpreted as encouraging. His hand moved downwards towards her breast. She was so astonished that it took her several seconds to realise what was happening and put a stop to it by standing up. He was at least fifteen years younger than she was, and surprise threw her completely off balance. She made such a mess of her reasons for refusing his dinner invitation that she had to let herself be bullied into accepting it.

"Good," he commented. "You need cherishing a bit, and I intend to do it."

His idea of "cherishing" her was dinner at a pretentious country house restaurant. The menu handed to her had no prices on it, and she doubted if Peter could really afford the sort of prices that must be marked on his. While they ate, he talked amusingly about a recent political scandal which had been inflated beyond reason by an unsuccessful attempt to suppress it. Normally she enjoyed his chatter, but not now—it reminded her of a tasteless courtship display by some rather conceited bird. He had not followed up his boldly sexual gesture, he was letting its message sink in and biding his time. Sound technique, she thought, he would leave making his next move till he thought she was waiting for it, wondering why it had not come.

As she knew to her cost, quite a lot of youngish men were attracted by the idea of a fling with an experienced older woman. But Peter did not strike her as that type, and if he had been enslaved by her charms, why on earth had her early warning system failed to detect the usual storm-signals long ago? Answer, because there had been no storm-signals, not the slightest hint that he fancied her. Why not? The answer was not flattering. He did not fancy her. He had some cold-blooded motive, his approach was part of some deep-laid scheme which had nothing to do with sex.

The time came to go home and she wondered what would happen when they got there. Nothing, to keep her dangling hopefully? A chaste kiss on the doorstep, to give her something to dream about? An attempt to get into the house, in the hope of hitting the jackpot in the bedroom? No. Nothing so crude, that was not the jackpot he was after. What was it? She had no idea.

When the moment arrived he settled for the kiss on the doorstep. But after the chaste salute on the cheek he came at her again and tried to deliver something more meaningful for her to think about.

She disengaged herself gently. "Peter, please don't start being silly."

"I'm not being silly, Celia love. You need someone to look after you."

"I'm not a mental defective, what d'you mean?"

He stood towering over her, very macho with his legs apart. "You can't run that huge business without a man to lean on. Why not lean on me?"

So that was it, the business was the real attraction, not her. Misreading her relationship with Bill, he had decided

121

that she fancied younger men and thought he could use his sex to fill the slot that Bill seemed to be vacating.

"You must be out of your mind," she snapped, and let herself into the house.

The urgent question was, had he tried to push Bill out of the slot he coveted by lying about the time he had passed Bill in the lane? Could he really be as evil as that? Probably, but she had to be sure. And she did not care how crudely she behaved to find out.

In the morning she opened up the nursery and let the staff in, then set off for Peter's place of work, the Government Horticultural Research Institute on the far side of Welstead. It was a sprawling mass of office and laboratory buildings of different periods. Was the laboratory that Peter worked in open late at night, and had he been working late on a certain evening a few weeks ago? She had no idea how to find out, but she had provided herself with an excuse for her visit by memorizing the name on the bottle of fungoid spray he had given her. As a way of getting into the building, she told the girl at the reception desk that she had come to enquire about a cure for cyclamen mite called AcNPV6.

The receptionist had never heard of it. Nor had various people she consulted on the telephone. A passer-by ventured an opinion that the V in the formula must stand for virus, and on the strength of that she was directed through a labyrinth of corridors to the virology department where she was received by Dr. Carling, the departmental head.

"You're quite right," he told her. "We are working on several derivatives of the parent virus, which is of course AcNPV, in other words *Autographa californica* nuclear polyhedrosis virus. Nothing's been published yet, may I ask how you came to hear of it?"

"A neighbour of mine who works here mentioned it to me. I have a small nursery business, and I'm having trouble with cyclamen mite."

"He's quite right, it's tailored to be specific against *Tarsonemus pallidus* in all its forms. But I'm afraid it won't be available for commercial use for several years yet."

Alarm bells began ringing in Celia's head. "You said it was 'tailored'. Does that mean it's a genetically engineered virus?"

"Yes, and we're still at the stage of safety tests in the laboratory. If it gets a clean bill of health we shall ask the relevant government departments and advisory bodies for permission to conduct a limited field experiment in an enclosed ecosystem out of doors, carefully netted to prevent any escape. When the risks have been assessed and the relevant authorities have decided that they're negligible, we'll be able to release it into the environment for general use."

"I'm sorry," said Celia in mounting panic. "It's been released into the environment already. Peter Verney gave me some to use on my cyclamen."

❧ SEVEN ❧

Carling stared at her. "Dr. Verney gave you some AcNPV6? How much?"

"Enough to treat about a thousand *Cyclamen libanoticum*. I assumed that he was a responsible scientist, and that anything he gave me would be perfectly safe."

"Where are these cyclamen of yours, in the open? . . . In a glasshouse, thank heaven for that. Were the ventilation lights open when you sprayed it on? . . . Kept them closed, did you, to maintain the humidity? Have they been opened since?"

"No, he told me to keep the humidity high for two days. I was going to open the lights tomorrow."

"We've been lucky, but it's still a major ecological crisis. The cyclamen will have to be destroyed and the glasshouse disinfected and fumigated. We'd better get on to that at once, and of course the incident will have to be reported to the Ministry. If the media get hold of it, there'll be hell to pay."

Celia was still numb with shock, but tried to gather her wits. "If you want to keep it from them, you'd better be careful who you send to clean up the mess. I have some very organic friends of the earth as neighbours, and they're even more terrified of genetic engineering than I am. If they see a van with the name of your organisation on it and a lot of disinfecting going on, they'll put two and two together and utter very public cries of horror, and the media will be at your throats in no time."

"Thanks for the warning, we'll do what we can. Well, at least you've caught our thief for us, Mrs. Grant. Our security people are turning the place upside down because a phial of the AcNPV6 culture went missing from the lab the other day, and it's not the first theft we've had."

"Yes. He gave me two batches of *Ambliseius mackenzii* earlier."

"For your cyclamen? *Ambliseius* wouldn't do them much good, but at least it's not an environmental risk. Why on earth did he do it?"

"He had personal reasons for wanting to ingratiate himself with me."

"Wanted a job at your nursery, did he? His contract with us runs out next month and we're not renewing it."

Yet more light dawned on Celia. The motive for Peter's indecently hasty wooing had become clear.

"Thank goodness you came forward, Mrs. Grant," Carling added. "What made you suspicious of him?"

"Various things. He claimed to have been working late at the laboratory on an occasion when I thought it couldn't be true."

"Quite right, it couldn't be, he doesn't work there any more. He was caught fudging his experimental results to prove a theory, and we transferred him to Documentation to get him out of the way while he works out his notice. But it's a case for summary dismissal now."

Celia rose to go. "How soon can you get a team to Archerscroft to clear up the mess?"

"I'll organise something for this afternoon, and meanwhile don't let anyone go in that glasshouse."

He opened the door for her and said to the secretary, "Ring Documentation and tell Dr. Verney I want to see him at once."

Back at Archerscroft she sent for Jenny Foster. "Ah,

Jenny. I've decided to throw out all those little Lebanon cyclamen in number three glasshouse. That mite has got too strong a hold, we'll have to write them off as a total loss."

"But that stuff of Dr. Verney's was doing rather well, Mrs. Grant. Have another look at them before you decide."

Celia pretended to consider, before telling her next lie. "No, those mites are much too dangerous," she said. "Unless we get rid of them once and for all, and disinfect the house, they'll metapause over the winter and we'll have the same trouble next year."

Jenny looked appalled, as well she might, at the prospect of several thousand pounds' worth of *C. libanoticum*, the result of much hard work, going down the drain.

"Without Bill we're too short-handed to tackle the job ourselves," she added, "so I've called in some outside people. They'll be here this afternoon."

The sight of Jenny reminded her of something else she had meant to arrange. "By the way, d'you know who's watering Joan Berridge's plants while she's away?"

"The old lady that lives next door."

"There are masses of them, all over the house. Would she welcome a bit of help?"

"Goodness yes, she's worried out of her mind about whether she's watering them right. One of the African violets died and she sort of went into mourning for it."

"Splendid, could you take over from her?"

Jenny hesitated. "I thought of offering to help, but I didn't want to seem nosy. You know what Joan's family are like. D'you think I should?"

"Yes, for a very naughty reason. I want that house searched, and I'd rather not get caught burgling it. So if you wouldn't mind—"

"Of course not, Mrs. Grant. What would I be looking for?"

"A book. You see, Joan Berridge used to send Bill little love-bouquets, based on the Victorian language of flowers—"

"Did she? Silly cow, I always knew she was a red-hot

126

furnace of love under all that fat. Fancy her fixing on gorgeous Mr. Wilkins though."

"The point is, she must have got the details of which flowers meant what from some book. When the police quizzed her about the love-bouquets, she said she hadn't sent them. I need the book to prove that she was lying. She's probably hidden it away, so it won't be easy to find. I thought if you don't mind, you could look for it when you go in to water."

"Of course, Mrs. Grant. Anything I can do to help get Mr. Wilkins off."

Celia's next concern was to make her peace with Bill. A phone call revealed that he wanted no visitors. Could she write? Certainly, if she wished. But it was a difficult letter to draft. She made two false starts and tore them up, and started again.

Dear Bill,

I owe you an abject apology. When you said you thought Peter Verney was "after" me, I didn't believe you, because I had seen no sign that he was interested in me sexually. He isn't, but he's lost his job at the laboratory and he decided that I, or rather the nursery, was going to be his next meal ticket. This only became clear last night, when he made an unbelievably crude approach. I suppose he was in a hurry to get fixed up before his contract ran out. Then he could tell me he'd resigned, "to help me run the business," instead of having to confess that he'd been fired.

Something else he did was quite unforgivable. He said he'd seen you coming home down the lane that night at a quarter to twelve, and this was of course a lie, intended to undermine your alibi and make me think you were guilty. I suppose the idea was that I'd fall in with his plans more easily if you were out of the way.

Now came the difficult bit.

I can't imagine how I came to take him seriously enough to ask you a question about the timing of the goat episode. I really am most awfully sorry, and don't know what came over me. Please can we be friends again, and don't despair. I'm doing everything I can to clear up the mess and get you out of that awful place soon.

Regards
Celia

As she addressed the envelope a shadow fell across her desk. She looked up and saw Peter Verney, standing just inside the office door.

"Go away, you squalid pest," she growled, "before I say something unladylike."

"Celia, let me explain."

"There's nothing to explain. As a scientist you're irresponsible. As a sex-athlete preying on older women you're a pathetic flop. As a liar about an innocent man's alibi you deserve to be cut into tiny pieces and fed to starving vultures, and I'd cheerfully do it if I had time."

"But Celia—"

"Don't interrupt. You said you were working late in the laboratory that night, but you can't have been. You were thrown out of the lab for faking your results. Where were you? In a pub?"

"No! If you must know, I went to the cinema in Welstead."

"And did you overtake Bill in the lane on your way home?"

"Of course, Celia, that's absolutely true."

"What time did the cinema come out? Don't tell me a lie, because I shall check."

"Ten fifteen or thereabouts. But Celia—"

"Don't interrupt. Did you come straight home?"

He hesitated.

"Don't invent anything, you'll be found out. Even if you say you were in a brothel I shall march in and ask."

He shrugged, but said nothing.

"So you drove straight home, and it was about ten thirty when you overtook Bill in the lane. That's the truth, isn't it?"

128

"Don't you see, I was trying to save you from yourself. He's obviously guilty and you were going round accusing everyone of giving false evidence against him. I had to stop you somehow, before you made yourself a laughing-stock in the village."

"Nonsense. Bill is not guilty and you deliberately tried to destroy my faith in him because you thought he was in the way of your greedy plans. Now get out of here. I shall behave in a civilised manner if we meet at Parish Council meetings or in other people's houses, and I hope you will too. Apart from that I shall try to forget the regrettable fact that you exist."

"Celia, I've been sacked from my job. Don't you care for me at all?"

"No, you overgrown would-be gigolo. Get out of here before I throw something at you."

She picked up some papers from her desk and pretended to study them. Peter stood looking at her for a moment, then went.

The party from the Institute arrived that afternoon, four workmen led by Dr. Carling himself. He took Celia aside. "We must try to avoid a public scandal. How much do your staff know?"

"Nothing," she said and repeated the cover story she had told Jenny.

"Good. The less they see the better, so could you send them home? You could say the spray we use is very toxic, and it's for their own safety."

The van they had brought had nothing written on it. When Jenny and the other girls had gone, she made them park it across the end of the glasshouse where the door was, so that what was going on inside could not be seen from over the Tidmarshes' fence. The clean-up operation began, and reminded Celia of grim police proceedings at the scene of a murder. Under Carling's supervision, her precious cyclamen were put in black plastic bags, pots and all, and taken out to the unmarked van by men trying not to look shocked, like policemen carrying bagfuls of decomposing human remains. The earth in the beds under the benches was condemned with horror as a hazard and removed in more plastic bags, and when the glasshouse had been emptied of everything, men in gas masks filled every corner of it with an evil-smelling spray.

All this activity had attracted the attention of the Tidmarshes. They had formed themselves into a spectators' gallery on their side of the fence, and expressed their disapproval loudly when the men began applying their spray to the outside of the glasshouse.

"Is this really necessary?" Celia asked nervously.

"I'm sorry, yes," said Carling. "There's a theoretical risk that the virus could have escaped through the ventilation lights or through overlaps in the glass."

A path along one side of the glasshouse received a drenching, and so did a long seedbed, fortunately empty, on the other. A patch of *Aster frikartii* growing a little further away narrowly escaped being denounced as a hazard, but a tray of the Archerscroft double primroses which someone had left near the glasshouse door joined the polluted cyclamen in the unmarked van. It was almost seven in the evening when the elaborate purification ceremonies were over and the team packed up to leave.

"I think you're perfectly safe now, Mrs. Grant," Carling assured her cheerfully. "I wouldn't try to grow anything for six months or so in the areas we've sprayed, but they'll be okay after that."

They went, leaving Celia to contemplate the loss of her lucrative cyclamen and the disruption of her nursery, and also to think of some cover story to tell the Tidmarshes, who were still manning the fence and demanding peevishly to know what was going on. On reflection she decided that half the truth plus a thumping lie would meet the case admirably.

"I've been taking precautions against an environmental risk," she told them, "after being taken in by an unscrupulous salesman. He supplied me with what I thought was a natural fungus like one of the *Verticilliums* for use against glasshouse pests. After I'd applied it I discovered something that he ought to have told me: the active principle of the fungus was a genetically engineered virus.''

The Tidmarshes greeted this with gasps of dismay.

''I know,'' Celia added hypocritically. ''The stuff he sold me is in general use and supposed to be perfectly safe, but I share your horror of genetic engineering and decided to destroy every trace of it before any harm was done.''

The Tidmarshes beamed. Evidently she was on the side of the angels after all. ''Do come in and have a glass of our home-made mead,'' said Wendy.

''How kind of you,'' said Celia, embarrassed by this undeserved approval. ''But I'm tired and absolutely filthy, some other time perhaps.''

She went to the office block to lock up, and glanced at her open desk diary to check her agenda for next day. To her dismay she saw that she had a dinner date in ten minutes' time for which she was about to be sensationally late.

The date was with a commuter and his wife who lived in one of the new executive houses, and were making valiant but mistaken attempts to integrate themselves into the village. On moving down from London they had become arch-conservationists, and treated Melbury as a museum-piece which they had a godsent mission to protect from the slightest taint of development, other than the executive estate in which they lived. The husband made a nuisance of himself on the Parish Council about footpaths and the wife baked cakes earnestly for all the village charities. Weeks ago, before the storm blew up, she had agreed reluctantly to dine with them, because yet another refusal would have looked too pointed. And now she had forgotten all about it, and it was far too late to make an excuse.

Making herself presentable in a rush, she drove to the raw new house in its pathetic little patch of garden, arriving well after the second round of drinks had been poured. She murmured an apology and was introduced. A minor television celebrity and his wife seemed to be the guests of honour. The other couple were neighbours of the host and hostess. But the spare man provided for her delectation turned out to be, horror of horrors, James Templewood, the colonel's son and Paul's elder brother.

He was a solicitor practising in London, and turned out to be a commuter-train contact of the host's, living three stations up the line. Had his father told him of her outrageous and impertinent attempt to question him about the Red Lion disaster? Or had her assault on the colonel's sensibilities been so traumatic that he had not brought himself to mention it, even to his son? James greeted her without the slightest trace of hostility, but he could have been bottling up fierce resentment to avoid spoiling the party. Wondering nervously about this, she downed a much-needed whisky as quickly as possible and they all sat down to an elaborate meal which no one but an upwardly mobile executive wife half out of her senses would have attempted to prepare and serve singlehanded.

James was next to her, and proved a more lively dinner companion than his father. He was going out of his way to make himself agreeable, and she began to think that the colonel must have kept his indignation to himself. Anyway, she was in a mood to take risks, and the opportunity was too good to let slip. Under cover of a long-winded anecdote from the celebrity she said to James, ''Tell me a bit about your brother Paul.''

''Why d'you ask?''

''I'm interested. It seemed such a tragic business. What sort of person was he?''

''His basic trouble was that he was terribly shy. As you can imagine, that didn't go down at all well in our family.''

''Was he frightened of your father?'' she asked.

''We both were. Him even more than me. Dad could make him stammer, just by looking at him.''

''But what was so frightening about him?''

''He wanted us to be tough, even as little boys. He'd rigged up an assault course in the garden that we had to go through, and there was a sort of youth club of village boys that he was toughening up too. I usually managed, but Paul was three years younger and he was a bit of a funk to put it crudely. There were awful scenes with Dad because he made a fuss about learning to swim, and Paul never went anywhere near water if he could help it. Dad couldn't understand how anyone could be like that. He had this magnificent war record, and I don't think he even knew what cowardice was.''

Celia pitied Paul deeply. To be the nervous son of a brave father would have been bad enough. But the colonel's nerve had failed at the crucial test and he was taking out his guilt on his sons, trying to make them what he had failed to be.

''Was Paul sound on the subject of girls and so on?'' she asked.

''What d'you mean?''

''As opposed to boys.''

''I used to wonder about that, but it's not the sort of thing you can ask your brother. He must have been okay I suppose, in the end there was that girl he got into trouble.''

So that's that, Celia thought. James was only eighteen when it happened and he believes what he was told, with Paul firmly cast as the father of Barbara's child. Or else he knows more and isn't telling.

The long television anecdote ended, and the conversation became general. When it got noisy enough, James murmured in her ear, ''Everyone in this room is agog to hear the ins and outs of your head gardener being held for murder, but they're too well bred to ask. Are you going to oblige?''

''I'd rather strip naked and dance on the table,'' she said and began quickly to talk about something else.

She woke at three in the morning and began racking her brains for some line of investigation to follow up. Nothing came, but James Templewood had filled in a useful piece of background. Was there anyone else she could persuade to gossip about the old days and perhaps give her a lead? Yes. Old Mrs. Wilson.

Mrs. Wilson's unmarried daughter had worked at Archerscroft till she died of cancer, leaving her elderly mother with no one to look after her. Celia had been instrumental in getting the old lady into a block of old people's flatlets in Welstead. Out of a sense of duty Celia visited her from time to time, and as the old lady's conversation consisted almost entirely of memories of the past, it would be easy to find out if she had anything useful to contribute.

The residents in the flatlets could have a few treasured possessions about them, and when Celia called in the morning the framed photograph she remembered from previous visits was there on the chest of drawers. It had been taken in Melbury, by the pool which supplied water to the paper mill. A group of boys in swimming trunks were sunning themselves on the grassy bank, with others in the water behind them. Several village worthies of the 'eighties were just recognisable in their teenage versions, notably Ron Tunney and Charley Englefield. Three figures in the background vaguely resembled the Pritchard brothers and Chris Wood.

The photograph provided an ideal introduction to the matter in hand. "It was took one very hot summer," the old lady explained. "There was a whole page of them photos in the paper, showing how people were keeping cool in the heat wave."

"Who are these two?" Celia asked, pointing to two youths in the foreground of the picture.

Mrs. Wilson took it from her and peered at it through her glasses. "That's Bertie Wood, and that's Jimmy Englefield, the brother of Charley that has the shop. Lovely boys they were, both of them."

And both killed by Paul Templewood. Celia recognised them now, from the pictures of the victims which had accompanied the *Gazette's* report on the Red Lion inquest. So when had the picture been taken?

"It was the summer before that dreadful thing happened," said the old lady, "and those two boys and a lot of others got killed."

"And that's why you've kept the photo?"

"No dear, it was because of him." She jabbed a finger at another figure, a much younger boy. "That's my grandson Derek, my Mary's eldest. Now he was a lovely boy, he really was. Only eleven when it happened."

But according to the *Gazette*, no one called Derek had been killed in the Red Lion shooting. So how and when did he die?

"He was drowned, dear. In the mill-race, not long after the man from the *Gazette* took that picture. My Mary took on terribly about it and no wonder, losing her husband and her boy like that within three months of each other. The floor in the butcher's shop was always spotless when her David had it, not like it is now with that Harrison that took it on afterwards. He was a lovely man too, her David was."

So Derek's father was David Black, the butcher who had been Paul's first victim. And Derek had died in the summer, almost three months before Paul shot his father.

"I often wonder how he'd have turned out if he'd lived," said the old lady with a break in her voice. "I know you're not supposed to have favorites, but he was the pick of all my grandchildren."

Celia looked at the photograph again. The camera had caught Derek at the last moment of bright childhood, before the onset of puberty had coarsened his features and dulled his mind with the urges of adolescence. To lose a child at that moment must leave an intolerable wound. When she looked up, Mrs. Wilson was weeping gently for Derek.

While Celia waited for her to recover, she looked at the photograph again. It was a glossy print, not a newspaper cutting. But there was something odd about it, and on looking more closely she saw what the oddity was: a bush growing near the river bank which somehow did not look natural, an odd-shaped blob rather than a bush. The glass of the frame made it difficult to be sure, but it looked as if the print had been retouched to obliterate something. One of the bathers? Why would the art department of the *Gazette* want to do that?

"You got this soon after your grandson was drowned?" she asked.

The old lady ruminated. "No. At first all I had was the cutting from the paper. But my cousin George Tunney, that's a nice man now, very kind and attentive since my Edward died, he saw this newspaper picture stuck in a frame on the mantelpiece, and he said wouldn't I like a proper picture to remember my Derek by, and the other boys in the picture that died in that terrible business. I said yes I would, so he took the newspaper picture away to show to the people at the *Gazette*, and he brought me this one instead."

Celia was fascinated. Was she quoting George Tunney accurately? If he had really spoken of remembering "the other boys in the picture that died in that terrible business," then the glossy print with something blotted out had been substituted for the newspaper cutting *after the disaster at the Red Lion*. Wanting to be quite sure of this, she put the question directly.

"Oh yes dear, it was after that. I think it was those other boys being killed put it into his mind."

Leaving the old lady to her thoughts, she drove to the newspaper offices. Clearly there would have to be another research session among the yellowing back files of the *Gazette*, and on this occasion Archerscroft would have to go to rack and ruin while she conducted a time-consuming trawl through July and August to find the right issue of the paper. But that could not be helped, and the sooner she got down to it the better.

She was lucky, and hit quickly on the right issue, at the end of July. The scene by the millpool was in the centre of a full page of pictures on the theme *How our readers kept cool in the heat wave*. The art department of the *Gazette* had not retouched the photo before publication. The printed version contained no suspicious-looking bush on the edge of the water, only another bather turning to face the camera. Celia recognised him at once. The thin, rather weak face had stared out at her before from the pages of the *Gazette*, among the photos illustrating the inquest story. It was Paul Templewood.

Why was it important that Paul should not be seen in the bathing party by the millpool? Or rather, why did it become important several months after the picture was published? The press cutting with him in it had been displayed on Mrs. Wilson's mantelpiece for months, and no one had been bothered. Then came the shooting at the Red Lion. Almost every copy of that week's *Gazette* had been used to wrap up fried fish or thrown out with the rubbish months ago, and no one remembered just who was in the picture. But Mrs. Wilson's copy with Paul in it was still on the mantelpiece for anyone to see. It had to disappear. But why?

According to James Templewood, his brother never went near water if he could help it. Had he been attracted to the millpool to meet boys his own age? Or because of the very hot weather? Had he been ordered to go there by his martinet of a father? In any case, his appearance at the millpool must have been a rare event. And someone was anxious that it should be forgotten.

Who? Puzzling over this, she was almost out of the building when she realised that she was not being thorough. A week or two after the picture was taken, Derek Black had been drowned. There would be an account of that in the paper. She must look it up before she left.

The story was at the bottom of a column, and quite short.

MELBURY BOY DROWNED

A verdict of accidental death was recorded at the inquest on eleven-year-old Derek Black, who was drowned last Saturday while swimming in the mill-race at Melbury Paper Mill. He had become trapped while attempting to swim under the millwheel.

According to the medical evidence, Black had suffered a severe head injury, probably the result of hitting the mill-wheel, and had apparently lost consciousness and drowned.

A number of older boys who were present at the time were questioned by the coroner. Asked why none of them had gone to Black's assistance, Simon Berridge said that they had all swum through the mill-race and under the mill, and were waiting for Derek to follow them. When he failed to do so they assumed at first that he had been afraid to plunge into the mill-race. By the time they realised that he was in difficulties, it was too late. He agreed with the coroner that swimming down the mill-race had been his idea, and that he had suggested it to the others in the form of a "dare." Charles Englefield and Albert Wood, who were neighbours of the Black family, said that although Derek was younger than the others, he was a strong swimmer and none of them had seen any reason why he should not attempt the swim if he wanted to do so.

Mr. Martin Brown, manager of the paper mill, stated that the company had allowed bathing in the pool above the mill during the hot weather. There was no warning notice about the danger of swimming over the weir and down into the mill-race, because it had not occurred to him that anyone would attempt to do so. If the accident had happened on a weekday, he would have seen what was happening from his office, and would have warned the boys of the danger.

There was no photograph of Derek in the paper, but she was haunted by the image of the alert little boy in the foreground of Mrs. Wilson's picture, and decided to visit the scene of his drowning. Feeling very much an intruder and hoping that neither of the Bradshaws would be about, she drove down the lane to the mill and stood on the footbridge over the weir. Behind her was the placid millpool where a group of boys, now men, had bathed and sunned themselves on the grass. In front was the huge mass of the mill, and beneath her feet the weir, where the water from the millpool crashed steeply down into the dark tunnel under the mill which housed the great wheel, still there but unused for over a century. What had Derek felt as he stood there, waiting to plunge in and follow the others through the tunnel and out into the river on the far side of the mill? Excitement? Fear of being thought too young to keep up with the gang? Terror and pride mixed as he slid off the footbridge into the dark water below?

She stood there for a long time, staring down into the

mill-race. Then she decided to look at the other end of the tunnel. This involved quite a walk, round the end of the mill building and through a passageway between it and a warehouse added on in modern times. When she emerged on the downstream side of the mill, where the water flowing underneath it joined the main river, she found that it was impossible to see into the tunnel from the bank, let alone up it as far as the wheel. She could imagine the group of boys climbing up on to the bank and wondering why Derek was being so slow, then realising that something was wrong and hurrying back round the mill to the footbridge and looking down on his body, jammed under the wheel.

Why had he been the last to face the "dare"? Why had not one of the older boys waited with him to see him through safely, then follow? Probably because they thought Derek was too young to be a member of the gang and did not expect him to attempt the swim.

Satisfied with this explanation, she drove home. But the thought of the brave little boy alone on the footbridge, determined to prove he was as tough as the rest of them, spoilt her appetite for her lunchtime bread and cheese. As the afternoon wore on, his tragic death loomed larger and larger in her thoughts, till she had to ask herself why it was haunting her so naggingly. Because she had got the story wrong? Surely not, it was perfectly straightforward. Putting it out of her mind, she concentrated on the real problem: why had Paul Templewood been edited out of the photo of the bathing party?

It baffled her all evening. She was getting ready for bed when the answer suddenly came. Stupid, stupid, she told herself, why didn't I think of that before? She began constructing a revised scenario of the fatal bathing party. Two people, not one, were standing on the footbridge, Derek and fifteen-year-old Paul Templewood. They were the last in the queue to swim the tunnel. They had hung back because they knew they would have to screw up their courage to face the ordeal, and did not want anyone watching them while they did it. The others assumed that Paul would look after Derek.

Paul is gazing down into the water, knowing that the village will brand him as a coward if he flinches. While he dithers, Derek Black is suddenly in the water. Does Paul have time to realise that his disgrace will be all the greater if he fails to do what an eleven-year-old child has just done? Probably not, for almost at once Derek has hit his head on something and is stuck under the millwheel.

Paul stares down at him. He knows what he ought to do, but cannot bring himself to do it. The shock of seeing Derek come to grief has unnerved him utterly. How can he plunge into the water and suffer the same fate as Derek? Instead, he turns tail and rushes off towards home.

In the end, the other boys come back to the footbridge to find out what has happened to Derek. Two of them get him out of the water somehow. He is unconscious. Probably one of them knows enough to try artificial respiration. Another goes to look for adult help. Perhaps someone sees Paul dashing uphill through the meadows in a panic, making for home. Anyway, they all remember that Paul was there with Derek till a few moments ago.

They are indignant. Why did Paul not go in after Derek and rescue him instead of running away like a coward? He is the son of Colonel Templewood the war hero, who has tried to dragoon the boys of the village into being as tough and brave as he is himself. What a let-down it will be for him to find that his own son is a coward. The village will laugh up its sleeve when they hear.

But someone—surely it must have been Simon Berridge?—has a better idea. They work it out in detail. When adult help arrives, none of them mentions that Paul was even there. And within a few days Paul begins to be desperately short of money.

❧ EIGHT ❧

Suddenly, a whole new landscape of ideas opened up. Here was a possible answer to the most baffling question of all: who had been blackmailing Paul Templewood and why? But if it was the right answer it raised another question. Blackmailing Paul would not have been possible unless all the boys who had swum in the mill-race agreed not to tell anyone that Paul had been there watching Derek drown. They all had to be in the conspiracy, but who were they? Charley Englefield the future shopkeeper, Bert Wood the dead brother of a future postman, and Ron Tunney the future traffic policeman and censor of Melbury's morals. Those three had been mentioned in the newspaper report, but there must have been others. Who were they? And how could she find out?

Next morning, after a whirlwind session in the office dealing with queries from workers in the packing shed and the frame yard, she was working away quietly on a batch of her special *Helleborus niger x corsicus* seedlings when it occurred to her that there was an obvious way of finding out what she wanted to know. Leaving Jenny Foster in charge, she drove back into Welstead and paid another visit to Mrs. Wilson, bearing by way of excuse an imposing Brunsvigia in full flower which she had taken out of stock.

When she had presented it and been thanked fulsomely, she got down to business.

"I couldn't get your Derek out of my mind. What a dreadful thing. He wasn't alone, was he, when it happened?"

"Oh no dear," said Mrs. Wilson. "He was with a lot of older boys. I blame them really for not looking after him."

"I'm sure you do. I would in your place."

"It's supposed to be over and forgotten now, but I've never really forgiven them for letting our Derek dive into that mill-race. I've remembered all their names."

"Have you really, Mrs. Wilson? Your memory's wonderful, could you tell me now who they were?"

"Let me see now. Well, to start with there was that Ron Tunney. He's a policeman now, minding everyone's business for them, but he was a proper tearabout then. Them two Englefield boys were just as bad, Jimmy who's dead and Charley who has the shop. And Simon Berridge, he was the worst of the lot."

"You'd think there were enough of them there to look after Derek," Celia remarked.

"Wait a minute, I haven't finished yet. The Pritchard boys were there too, Bob and Pat, and Bert and Chris Wood, and Peter Berridge's two boys, Dick who was killed and Andy who has the garage. And there was someone else, who was it? Oh yes, a rather stupid boy from over at Stone Cross, called William Gurney."

Eleven boys, Celia reflected on the way back to Melbury. It was a much bigger conspiracy than she had suspected. Seven of the conspirators were still alive, grown men now with a guilty secret, no wonder the village had gone tight-lipped. And the death-roll showed that Paul had not lashed out at random with his shotgun. He had picked his victims carefully with vengeance in mind, killing four of his black-mailers, Bert Wood, Jimmy Englefield, Bill Gurney and Dick Berridge, and wounding two more, Simon Berridge and Pat Pritchard. He would probably have picked off the remaining five if they had not taken cover in time. But the only adult casualty did not fit into that pattern. If Paul's motive was vengeance, why had his first victim been David Black, the father of the boy he had left to drown?

The problem nagged her throughout a hard afternoon's work at Archerscroft. She could find no solution.

There was a meeting that evening in the village hall, to organise a campaign against a developer's plans to dump a huge new town, complete with "leisure facilities," between Melbury and the next village four miles away. She would have to attend, it was the sort of Melbury occasion when absence would mean a black mark, a thing she could not afford in her present situation vis-à-vis the village.

The meeting provided the usual mixture of lawyers' common sense from the platform and fiery defiance from the floor, with the newcomers from the executive estate among the most vocal. The riddle of David Black's killing still obsessed her, she had to talk to it over with someone. During the coffee session afterwards she decided, at the risk of a rebuff, to approach Jack and Ann Hammond.

"I've made some very odd discoveries," she announced. "Could I tell you about them and see how you react?"

Jack Hammond looked doubtful.

"Been rummaging in the skeleton-cupboard, have you?" said Ann. "You know I don't approve."

"Please," Celia begged. "I promise not to pry behind the screen of medical etiquette, but I'm bursting with information and must tell someone."

They were embarrassed, but seemingly decided it would be too unfriendly to refuse.

"This coffee tastes of old dishcloths," said Ann. "Let's go home and have a proper drink."

Over a stiff whisky in the Hammond's vast Georgian drawing room, she told them what she thought had really happened after Derek Black was drowned in the mill-race.

"What airy-fairy codswallop," Ann commented when she had finished. "Nothing but wishful thinking, to get your gorgeous gardener freed."

Celia ignored her and turned to Jack. "Ann says you

always thought there was something odd about the shooting at the Red Lion, something you didn't understand. Could you be more definite?"

"Don't, Jack," said Ann. "You'll only encourage her."

"Stop being such a shrew," Celia told her. "Come on, Jack, be a sport."

"I can't be very definite. It was mostly a creepy feeling that the whole story hadn't come out. The village was clamming up on us, like it does sometimes when it's got something to hide."

"Nonsense, Jack," Ann insisted. "They'd a good reason for going quiet, Paul had massacred the flower of Melbury's youth, they were all shook up. Celia's nonsense doesn't hang together. Paul wasn't shooting at random, she says, he was picking off his blackmailers one by one. Answer me this, Celia. Why was David Black the first to cop it? He was one of nature's gents, blackmailing teenagers wasn't his line at all."

"That's the big puzzle," Celia admitted. "But according to the evidence at the inquest Black said something as Paul went past him into the Red Lion. Nobody heard what it was, but it could have been something Paul took amiss, and that set off the crisis."

"I happen to know what David said to Paul," said Jack, "and it was perfectly harmless. It was only . . . oh!"

He broke off.

"Jack, what is it?" Ann demanded.

"I've just realised. Paul had been shooting very badly all morning, and at the last stand by the millpool he was all over the place. And what Black said to him was 'Didn't do very well down there by the mill, did you, Master Paul?' "

They digested this in shocked silence.

"And David Black was poor little Derek's father," said Celia, "so it wasn't a harmless remark, because of a double meaning that he didn't intend. Paul was well over the edge with worry and he misunderstood. He thought the blackmailers had told Black the story, and Black was taunting

144

him with having stood by while his son drowned."

Jack was still looking shocked. "I wondered at the time why no one at the inquest mentioned what Black had said. That was one of the things that puzzled me, but I see now."

"You were there at the shoot, then?" Celia asked.

"No, I was summoned from my surgery afterwards to deal with the carnage."

"Then how did you know what Black had said?"

"Simon Berridge told me while I was trying to save his eye, and I got much the same thing from Pat Pritchard. At that stage they thought the whole business started because Black had annoyed Paul by making this mildly critical remark about his shooting."

"But as soon as they'd recovered from the shock," Celia reasoned, "they saw why the remark had triggered Paul off, and decided to keep quiet about it. And at the inquest, they all agreed that Black had said something, but they all managed not to have heard what it was."

"Typical village behaviour," Jack murmured.

"I enjoy guessing games, this is fun," Ann broke in. "But it's all up in the air. You can't even prove that Paul was there when Derek was drowned."

"Well, there's the little matter of Mrs. Wilson's photo," Celia pointed out, "the one of the bathing party. How do we explain the two versions of it? For three months it was perfectly okay for her to have the press cutting with Paul in it on her mantelpiece. After the shooting at the Red Lion it isn't okay at all, and a glossy print with him blotted out has to be substituted. Why? Because it's suddenly become important not to remind anyone that Paul had ever been near the millpool. The version with him in it might have started people thinking."

"What they think doesn't matter a hoot," Ann objected. "Derek was alive when the photo was taken. Nobody's going to say, 'Ah, Paul was there then, so he must have been back at the pool later, when Derek drowned.'"

"I don't agree," Celia argued. "Remember, Paul was a coward about swimming. As a rule he wouldn't go near water. But it was a very hot summer. His father probably told him to go on down to the millpool and not be a sissy, and he couldn't think of an excuse. It was probably the first time he went there, and as far as anyone but the blackmailers knew, it was the last.''

"Far-fetched," Ann snorted.

"If you've got a bad conscience," Celia argued, "and are terrified of being found out, you cover your tracks and get rid of any clue that might start people thinking about your crime.''

"But why d'you wait for weeks before you switch the photos?" Jack asked her.

"Because you aren't really frightened of being found out till after the shooting at the Red Lion. The police have moved in, there will be an inquest. When the police start asking what got Paul into such a murderous state, they will soon find out that he's been blackmailed. If they discover who the blackmailers were, eleven teenage boys will be held morally responsible for causing a massacre in which five people died and two more were wounded. What are they to do? Keep their heads down and their mouths shut and hope for the best.''

"This is a damn silly guessing game," said Ann.

"Perhaps, but let me go on. Suddenly a miracle happens, and saves them. Another blackmail suspect has been produced to rescue them, like a rabbit out of a hat. Barbara Berridge announces that Paul is the father of her child.''

"Oh!" said Jack sharply.

"Whether she's telling the truth is an open question," Celia went on. "But don't worry, I know this is the point where you hide behind a barricade of medical etiquette, and I shan't ask you for the answer to that one. Instead, let's ask ourselves why the photo-switching was done by the next generation up, Ron Tunney's father.''

Both the Hammonds were trying to hide mounting alarm. Neither spoke so she supplied the answer herself. "Let's suppose that Ron, or perhaps George's nephew Simon, confessed to George and asked him to protect them from exposure. George Tunney's reaction is to send his niece straight into a trap. He knows what the boys have done, and foresees that as soon as Barbara says Paul was the child's father, she'll become the prime blackmail suspect and the boys will be in the clear. He's her guardian, she and Simon have been living with the Tunneys since their parents died. But he doesn't do what any decent adult would have done. He doesn't tell her firmly to keep her mouth shut and stay out of trouble. Is that believable?''

"No," said Jack in a shocked voice.

"So we have to assume that George Tunney didn't find out the truth till after the inquest. And what was his reaction? To clear his niece, and tell everyone who the real black-mailers were? No. He switched Mrs. Wilson's photographs to protect the boys and sacrificed her. Why?''

There was no answer from the Hammonds.

"He couldn't afford to let the real story come out," she went on. "He had to protect the boys to protect the real father of Barbara's child. Why did Barbara tell the inquest it was Paul? She could perfectly well have kept quiet, but she didn't. She was lying to divert the village's suspicion from someone else.''

The Hammonds were still silent, too shocked to react. After a long pause Ann said, "This is your fault, Jack you fool. I knew we'd end up here if you listened to her.''

"I have made no comment," said Jack. "And I don't intend to make one.''

Suddenly Ann rounded on Celia in a whirlwind of fury. "You intend to dredge up all this mud? And throw it at people who've been leading honest respectable lives for years? You can't prove any of it, if you bring up all this filth in court it won't help you to get your precious gardener cleared. The village was at sixes and sevens for years after that awful business, it took them ages to get over it. I've worked hard ever since we came here to hold things together and keep the village on an even keel. Have you thought what you'll be doing to Melbury if you rake it all up again?''

"The village is protecting the person who killed Simon

Berridge," said Celia. "And I can't help it if they have to take the consequences."

In bed that night, she lay awake for a long time, looking for flaws in her reasoning, but finding none.

If Paul had really been the father of Barbara's child, medical etiquette would not have prevented Jack Hammond from telling her so, and rebuking her for talking nonsense. Instead they had both reacted with horror to what she was suggesting, in a way which made it clear that the "mud" she had dredged up was real.

Who was the father, if not Paul? Another teenager who spotted that Paul's death gave him an "out," and persuaded Barbara to lie? If that was it, would George Tunney have gone on protecting the boys, and sacrificed her rather than let the truth about that come out?

Why did Barbara have to say anything about the child's paternity? To divert suspicion away from the obvious suspect. Who was the obvious suspect? Someone with enough influence over her to browbeat her into telling a lie, and the strongest possible motive for making her tell it. There was only one candidate who fitted this specification. It had to be him, but as Ann Hammond had insisted again and again, the proof was still lacking.

What was the next step? After a lot of turning and tossing, she decided to make a frontal attack on Barbara, preferably in the daytime when her husband would be busy in the mill. Next morning, after she had shopped in the village, she turned into the lane leading down to it, and found Barbara on all fours in the garden of the mill house, weeding the border that Celia had helped her design.

"Hello, Barbara. This is going to look rather good when it gets established."

Barbara looked up, not pleased to see her. Evidently Bradshaw had reported to her on Celia's vain attempt to get the truth out of him. "Oh, hello," she said awkwardly, and searched around for something more to say. "I suppose I could fill up the gaps with annuals, but it didn't seem worth while.''

"No, far better to leave the permanent planting all the room it's going to need.''

They fenced for a little longer with embarrassed small talk about the garden. Then Celia said, "I've something I want to discuss with you. Could we go inside?''

Barbara froze at once. "Is it about that business?''

"I'm afraid so, yes.''

Barbara squatted gawkily on her heels beside the border she had been weeding. "I don't want to talk about it. It's all over and done with and I want to forget it.''

"It isn't over and done with. D'you know why your brother was killed? Because he was threatening to tell a barful of beer drinkers who had fathered your baby.''

She looked panic-stricken. "So you say.''

"It's the truth. And he was killed to shut his mouth by the baby's father. An innocent person has been arrested in his place. Are you really prepared to let your uncle George get away with that after what he did to you?''

Barbara gasped and went beetroot red. "What d'you mean?''

"You know perfectly well what I mean.''

She was in shock. Tears of anger welled up. "Who told you?''

"No one. I worked it out for myself.''

She began to whimper like a slapped child. "Go away, Celia. It's no business of yours.''

"It is my business, and I'm not going away. He killed Simon, and he's letting Bill Wilkins take the blame for it. I'm not having that. How old were you when he started abusing you? Seven? Eight? Nine?''

Barbara blocked her ears. "Stop it, Celia. I can't talk about it. Even thinking about it makes me feel dirty.''

"And letting Bill Wilkins be jailed for a crime he didn't commit makes you feel clean?''

"I can't help that. All that matters is, no one must know what happened to me.''

149

She was lying on her face in the grass now, and sobbing wildly. Celia went on trying to reason with her for a little longer but it only made her more hysterical.

"If you don't go away, Celia," she shouted, scarlet with anger, "I shall fetch Ted from the office to throw you out."

Reviewing progress on the way back to Archerscroft, Celia was depressed. Child abuse was a traumatic experience for the victim, and she had not expected cosy girlish confidences. But blocked ears and hysteria were more than she had bargained for. The confession she had extracted was valueless. Barbara would deny that she made it however hard she was pressed. The only plus of the interview was confirmation that George Tunney was guilty. The long, tortuous chain of reasoning was correct.

Back at Archerscroft, Peter Verney was waiting for her in her office.

She glared at him. "I told you to keep out of my sight."

"I know you did, Celia, but you're not Catherine the Great of all the Russias, and I decided it was time we had a little talk."

"There's nothing to talk about."

"Oh but there is. You owe me an apology, Celia."

"Oh, do I? I'd rather apologise to an uneven paving stone for being tripped up by it."

"I helped you with your pest control problem, and you thanked me by getting me thrown out of my job."

"What job? It was going to end in a month anyway."

"I know, but I've lost a month's salary. That's why you owe me an apology. A money apology, I hasten to add."

She was outraged, but on reflection not surprised. "Getting money out of a stone would be child's play compared to me."

"In that case," he said, "I don't think my conscience will let me go on suppressing my evidence against Wilkins."

She was appalled, but tried not to show it. "Any nonsense of that kind from you and you'll never get another job in this neighbourhood, because my revelations will reduce your shady character to very unsavoury shreds."

"I'm moving on anyway. Before I go I shall dismiss your remarks airily as the malicious ravings of a discarded mistress." He picked up her handbag from the desk and opened it. "I'm a bit short of cash, so I'm helping myself to some on account. There's forty pounds here, that will do nicely. 'Bye now, think about what I've said. I'll be seeing you."

Celia did not protest when he took the money, and let him have the last word. It was good policy to let him think she was weakening. He would hold his hand and say nothing as long as he had hopes of getting money out of her. She would string him along for a week or two, till after the committal proceedings at least. Anything rather than let him add his lying voice to the attack on Bill's alibi.

The best way of heading him off would be to get the Tidmarshes to change their evidence about the time when the goat was killed. She seemed to be in high favour with them after her horrified purge of the genetically engineered virus, and had enough cards in her hand now to make the attempt worth while, so she rang them. Wendy, who took the call and received her invitation to come over for a drink that evening, was more ecstatic than the occasion required, but insisted that Celia should come to them, not vice versa. This had a double disadvantage. She would have to drink home-made concoctions of unknown potency, and if the going got rough she would have to be rude to the Tidmarshes in their own house. But there was no help for it. As soon as the nursery closed, she changed into an appropriately casual pair of slacks and went across.

The smallholding was looking as disorganised and scruffy as ever, and a veronica she had sold them was struggling for life in a disused bucket beside the front door. The Tidmarshes welcomed her warmly into their sordid and uncomfortable kitchen, settled her on a half-disembowelled sofa with a glass of fiery ginger wine, and prepared for conversation.

It soon became clear why she had been welcomed so warmly. Melbury was an unfriendly place, was it not? They had been here a year, and still knew no one. How long had

Celia lived in the village? Five years? Was she still treated as an outsider?

Celia was very willing to join the Tidmarshes as a fellow-pariah in the Melbury doghouse if it would help get Bill released. "We're in the same boat, aren't we? I'm really a shopkeeper like the Englefields and Harrison, the butcher. But I'm not accepted into their world, and at the same time I don't quite fit in with the gentry. You're the same. We're both of us neither one thing nor the other."

"Oh, we don't aspire to being noticed by the gentry," said Tidmarsh on a note of superior mockery. "People who can bear to live in those pretentious executive houses can hardly be worth knowing."

"Oh dear me no, they must be dreadful bores," Wendy added. "We've much more in common, though they seem to think otherwise, with the ordinary, humble cottagers in the Summerfield estate."

Celia refrained from saying that the ordinary humble cottagers regarded the Tidmarshes and their alternative husbandry as Melbury's funniest joke for years. More important, she had just been given the opening she needed.

"I don't think they've singled you out specially for the cold shoulder," she said. "The village treats everyone like that. Underneath the surface it's a very tightly organised little community, very inward-looking. It doesn't discuss its affairs with outsiders."

"What sort of affairs?" asked Wendy.

"Well, an old woman was murdered for her savings about ten years ago. The police couldn't get evidence and there probably wasn't enough to prosecute, but they all knew who had done it and they kept their mouths shut."

"How sinister," said Tidmarsh. Wendy shivered deliciously.

"There was another case before that," Celia continued, and told them an earthy story, to which they listened with round-eyed relish, of drowning, blackmail and incest in the long distant past.

The time had come for the punch line, and she made no

attempt to sound casual. "I think you should know that this story had a sequel the other day. On the evening Simon Berridge was killed he was in the Red Lion, very drunk and quarrelsome, and he threatened to name the father of that unfortunate girl's child. The father was there in the pub, knowing that unless Berridge was silenced, he would stand publicly accused of incest. So after closing time he killed Berridge and dumped him in the river."

"Oh!" cried Wendy in dismay.

"Are you sure of this?" asked Tidmarsh.

"Quite. I suspect that half the village knows who killed him and why. It'll be the usual story of nobody having seen or heard anything, or knowing the whys and wherefores. Meanwhile an innocent man has been arrested on trumped-up evidence, and the humble cottagers will look on calmly while he's tried for an offence he didn't commit."

There was a long silence.

"Having your goat killed must have upset you horribly," Celia added. "But if you were so upset that you missed that interesting broadcast, you had another chance to hear it when it was repeated the next day."

After another long silence, Tidmarsh said, "This is very awkward."

"It places us in an embarrassing position," Wendy agreed.

"Quite," said Celia. "But I'm sure upright people like yourselves would find it even more awkward and embarrassing to let an innocent man be convicted of a crime he didn't commit."

She watched the thoughts racing through their minds. If they offended her, it would be the end of the break-out from social isolation which she seemed to offer. On the other hand, it would be humiliating to admit that they had avenged their slaughtered goat by lying about the time of its death. Was there a graceful way out of the dilemma?

Presently Tidmarsh found one. "As usual, it is the police force which is really to blame."

Ferris, he explained, had told them that Bill claimed to

have shot the goat at about ten thirty. But according to Ferris that was a lie, and he invited them to help him prove it by giving him a later timing. After a lot of bullying from Ferris, who had insisted that Bill was guilty, they had yielded to pressure and complied. In retrospect, they felt that they had been too severe on Bill in the matter of the goat. Its behavior had certainly been anti-social, and they had been wrong to leap to the conclusion that a man capable of shooting a goat must automatically be guilty of a much more serious crime. Basically this was yet another case of Britain's near-fascist police collecting evidence by dishonest, underhand means in order to secure convictions.

Celia did not share the view, which they went on to expound, that the Sussex constabulary were among the oppressive public bodies responsible for all the ills of human society, nor could she accept that it was the fault of the police if witnesses gave false evidence from motives of revenge. But she was prepared to share the Tidmarshes' opinion of Detective-Inspector Ferris, and said so.

"What time did the goat business really happen?" she asked them.

They consulted each other. "Around half past ten," said Tidmarsh.

Questioned further, they said they would be willing to give formal evidence to this effect, though they insisted on incorporating an allegation that their original statements to Detective-Inspector Ferris had been extracted from them under pressure. This result was all the more delightful to Celia because it was bound to infuriate Ferris, and she went home feeling much more cheerful.

Next morning she paid a visit to Bill, who had received her letter and was as contrite as she was about their quarrel. The news that the Tidmarshes had repented and changed their evidence made him almost cheerful, and her account of her discoveries brought back some of the old excitement of the chase.

"But you can't prove nothing, can you?" he asked anxiously.

"No, but I intend to try."

"Oh but how, Celia?"

"Joan Berridge must have seen George Tunney attacking Simon that night in her front garden. I think I could batter the truth out of her if I could find her. But where is she, Bill? Where do I begin looking? My brain's addled, let me pick yours."

"Oh Celia, them two old lags yakking away in the cell have sent me bonkers, I got no brain left."

"Oh yes you have, so come along. The first puzzle is her state of mind. Did she disappear of her own accord, to avoid having to answer awkward questions from me? Or has Tunney whisked her out of the way against her will because she's been saying she wants to tell the truth? You know her better than I do, what's your guess?"

"I dunno. She's that scatty, it could be either, or both at once, or even turn and turn about, one in the morning and the other in the afternoon."

"If she's a free agent it's hopeless, she could have gone to ground anywhere, with a friend or distant relative miles away."

"Oh yes, Celia, but if she's been kidnapped it's a problem for Tunney, where is he to put her? There's not many places."

"In their spare bedroom on the Summerfield estate? Difficult. There are only two of them to supervise her, and those council houses are very close together. She'd only have to scream and the neighbours would get inquisitive, Melbury isn't West Beirut."

"Tunney's got relations," Bill pointed out. "He could have got some of them to take her in."

"Okay, but what happens when she says she wants to go home? What story does he tell them, to justify keeping her locked up? I don't think that's on."

"Some barn away in the fields, then," Bill suggested. "And they take her food twice a day."

"Leaving her unattended except at mealtimes? Not practical. Besides, there are no isolated barns left, they're all luxury barn conversions with two bathrooms and a Jacuzzi."

"So she's not a hostage because there's nowhere for her to be one."

"Yes, damn it. And that means she disappeared into the blue of her own accord, and we have no means of tracing her."

"No. Wait, Celia. There's something wrong with this." He shut his eyes and concentrated. "I think I got it now. How long's she been away?"

Celia calculated. "Ten days at least."

"Then we got it wrong somehow. Them plants. It's not credible, she'd never leave her precious plants that long of her own accord."

"Are you sure, Bill?"

"Dead sure. When a person's got no children they fix on something, a dog or a cat that can't be left. With Joan Berridge it's house plants that would miss her if she weren't there to talk to them."

"You're right, why didn't I think of that? I caught her at it once at the nursery, chatting up a trayful of primula seedlings. But if she dotes on her plants so, why hasn't she reappeared? I suppose she could be dead, like Simon. That would be a way of keeping her quiet, but I doubt it somehow. Another killing without you around to be blamed for it would take a lot of explaining away, so let's assume she's alive. I suppose Tunney could threaten her with death, torture or whatever if she talked, that would scare her out of her wits, such as they are. But where is she?"

They brooded silently for several minutes.

"How about this?" Bill suggested. "She's with relatives who've been told some story, not the true one, to give a reason for locking her up. She's gone off her rocker, say, and she's having delusions, and they better keep a sharp look-out or she'll be out in the road in her bra and panties. And if she says anything out of turn, they're not to take no notice, it's just the delusions."

"Bill, that was very clever of you. You weren't to know

156

this, but it's quite a credible story to tell. According to Ann Hammond, there's insanity in her family."

"That's it then. Tunney has sent her home to be locked up with her mad aunties, so she don't disgrace her in-laws by behaving silly in the village."

"Bless you, Bill. Now at least I've an idea about where to start looking. That was quite like old times, wasn't it?"

For the first time since his arrest, he gave her a broad grin.

Soon after she got back to the nursery, Jenny Foster came into the office and dumped a book in an elaborate Victorian binding on her desk. "Here you are," she said. "I think it's what you want."

"Oh bless you, Jenny. Where did you find it?"

"Top of Joan's spare room wardrobe, hidden under a suitcase."

"Clever you. How did you manage to get rid of the old lady?"

"She stood there like she always does seeing I didn't pinch anything, and I watered slower and slower and I fiddled around picking off dead leaves and teasing up the earth in the pots, and she began to look as if she never wanted to see me or a pot plant again. In the end she remembered she'd a cake in the oven and could we finish later. So I said no, I'd be busy later so would she like to do all the ones on the stairs herself, and remember that the maidenhair ferns needed a lot of water from the top and the African violets needed very little from the bottom, and be sure to pick off all the dead leaves from the streptocarpuses, and unless she did everything right the whole lot would die. So she looked sick as a cat with the chickenpox, but she was scared to do the watering herself in case she killed the lot, and if she didn't go home she'd be in mourning for a burnt cake. So in the end she left me to finish and lock up, and I had a good look round and found it."

She thanked Jenny warmly and took the book home to study over her lunch. It was John Ingrams' *Flora Symbolica* published in 1864, and there was an inscription on the title page: *Emily Hurcomb, for her birthday. 5th July 1873*.

It seemed to be a compilation of earlier books about the language of flowers, and gave alternative meanings when the previous authorities contradicted each other. For example, rosemary was listed under its French meaning, derived from de la Tour, as "Your presence revives me." But its Shakespeare-based meaning of "Remembrance" was also given. There was no doubt that this was the book used to compose the floral messages of love and hate which had been dumped on Bill's draining board, for the red tulip, the heliotrope, and the ranunculus and the mallow all had erotic meanings entered against them.

One problem remained. How was she to prove that the book belonged to Joan Berridge? By putting it back on top of her spare room wardrobe and telling the police it was there? Clumsy, and subject to deliberate human error if Ferris was the policeman involved. Who was Emily Hurcomb? If she was an ancestress of Joan Berridge the problem was solved, the inscription on the flyleaf showed who it belonged to. But was she? Who would know?

Ann Hammond, obviously. She rang her. "What was Joan Berridge's maiden name?"

"Celia, I'm not helping you with your enquiries. I don't approve."

"Oh, come on. I shall find out from someone, so why not you? Was it Hurcomb by any chance?"

"Since you know, why ask me?"

Roger Stevens had been in court all morning, but agreed to see her for a few minutes at two. When she told him about her success in persuading the Tidmarshes to change their story, the cheerful smile with which he confronted disaster was replaced by gloomy lawyerlike caution.

"You mean, they're prepared to swear affidavits that the goat was shot an hour earlier? But that gives our client an alibi."

"Quite. I'm afraid you'll have to face the fact that he's innocent."

158

"Could it be said that you put improper pressure on the Tidmarshes to change their evidence?"

"I doubt it. They propose to say in their affidavit that the police pressurised them into telling lies in their original statement."

"Oh no, that would antagonise the police. Most unwise."

"Ferris is antagonised already. You'll have to let them say it if they want to. They think, wrongly, that it will stop people suspecting that they lied to punish Bill for shooting their goat."

His gloom seemed to deepen. "When witnesses change their story, their credibility is open to attack."

"I daresay, but could you take affidavits from them as soon as possible? And here's something else I'd like you to look at." She passed John Ingrams' *Flora Symbolica* across the desk to him. "It belongs to Mrs. Berridge, Simon's widow. Remember, she denied having sent language-of-flowers messages to Bill. The meanings of all the flowers she sent him are in it. It was found in her house, hidden away on top of a wardrobe."

Stevens looked mildly horrified. "You mean, you stole it?"

"I borrowed it. If I ever find her I shall brandish it under her nose and call her a liar."

"Can you prove it's hers?"

She opened it at the inscription on the flyleaf. "Hurcomb was her maiden name."

"This could come in quite useful, Mrs. Grant. She'll be a key witness for the prosecution. When we present the defence case, counsel can use it to attack her credibility."

Celia was utterly dismayed, and said so, at the thought of Bill spending months cooped up in overcrowded cells waiting to be tried. If there wasn't enough evidence to get the charge against him dropped at the committal stage, couldn't they make another attempt to get him bail?

"I'm afraid not, Mrs. Grant. If he hadn't attacked his cell-mate like that we could try, but as it is—no, I'm sorry. We haven't a chance."

So that was that. She had less than a week before the committal proceedings in which to assemble cast-iron evidence that there was no case to answer. She would do it, or burst a blood vessel in the attempt.

At all costs she must find Joan Berridge. Could Tunney have had her shut away by her own family alongside her feeble-minded mother? Perhaps, but would he have trusted anyone outside his own family not to ask awkward questions? Relations of his own were more likely, but what relations did he have? Who could she ask? Not Ann Hammond, she had gone sulky and unhelpful. How about Mrs. Wilson? She was a storehouse of local lore and family history, and she was a relative of George Tunney's. Deciding that she was the best bet, Celia called there on her way home, on the excuse that she had left her umbrella somewhere, and wondered if it was at Mrs. Wilson's.

On entering the tiny living room she noticed at once that the photograph of the bathing party at the millpool was no longer on view. This was disconcerting, because she had been trying to invent an excuse to borrow it and have a copy made for use in evidence. She asked as casually as possible where it was.

"It's funny you should ask that, dear. My cousin George has got it."

"Oh? Why did he want it?"

"Simon's in it, his nephew that was killed the other day. He remembered I'd got the picture and he asked if he could take it and have a copy made. George must have been fonder of Simon than I thought, while he was alive they didn't seem to get on. I told him you'd been ever so interested when you saw it."

Damn, Celia thought. George Tunney had rumbled her, he must have taken alarm at her interest and put the photograph out of her reach. From now on he would be watching every move she made, and doing his best to trip her up.

But what relatives did he have, and did any of them sound like potential gaolers? "How do you and George Tunney come to be cousins?" she asked, to start Mrs. Wilson off.

This and a few more questions released a rich outpouring of genealogical information, involving uncles in Canada, second cousins in Tunbridge Wells, married sisters up north. Celia was soon completely lost as Mrs. Wilson raced up and down family trees from the nineteen-twenties to the present day, without always making it clear whereabouts in time she was.

"And then there are George's Hurcomb in-laws over at Ickfield," she said.

Celia was astonished. "You mean, he married into that family too, as well as his nephew Simon? Kathleen Tunney was a Hurcomb?"

"Of course, dear, didn't you know? She was the best of the bunch, they're a poor lot, and there's madness in the family. Too many cousins marrying each other, I suppose."

"But Joan Berridge is a Hurcomb too," said Celia.

"Yes. Simon should never have married that stupid lump. It was a shotgun wedding that turned out to be a false alarm."

This altered everything. Where better could George Tunney hide Joan Berridge away than with his wife's family? It was Joan's own family too, and it would take in its stride allegations that she was mentally disturbed. Celia tried to find out more about the Hurcombs, but Mrs. Wilson clearly disapproved of them. She would only repeat that they were a poor lot, that there were a great many of them, and that one of Joan's aunts had gone to the bad.

Eager to follow up this lead as quickly as possible, she drove straight to Lewes to consult the Ickfield section of the electoral register at the council offices and note down the names and addresses of all the Hurcombs who lived there. Mrs. Wilson was right, there were a lot of them. A family of four lived at Ickfield Stores and Post Office. Two couples lived in what seemed from the address to be a council estate, but one of them had a son who would be eighteen and entitled to vote later in the year, and an inquisitive teenager would be an awkward witness of an allegedly mad relative's imprisonment. There were two

Hurcomb women living together in something called Elm Close, and one more couple at Rose Villa in the High Street who had a Mrs. Bishop registered at the same address. Having noted all this, she drove on to Ickfield and called at the vicarage.

She was making enquiries, she said, on behalf of an American family called Hurcomb, who had emigrated from Sussex early in the nineteenth century and wanted to trace their English relatives. The vicar, a youngish man, was eager to help. "There are a lot of Hurcombs buried in the churchyard. Come along, I'll show you."

They were all there, in the shadow of the fourteenth-century church, including Emily, the owner of John Ingrams' book on the language of flowers. Celia feigned interest in the gravestones and took a few notes, then asked about the living members of the family.

"Well, there's James Hurcomb and his wife, they run the village shop. James's brother's a garage mechanic, he lives down on the housing estate, and their older boy and his wife are quite near them. Then there are two unmarried cousins, women in their seventies. You could try them for reminiscences, one of them's okay but the other's a bit simple. Oh, but wait a minute. I think your best bet would be an elderly couple called Hurcomb who live farther up the High Street, on the other side. I'm not sure if they're related to the other lot, but they're both getting on for ninety so their memories go back a long way."

"Goodness, and they live alone?" Celia asked, mindful of the Mrs. Bishop registered under the same roof.

"No, there's a daughter who used to be a nurse, divorced I think, who moved in to look after them when she retired. If you go to the shop and ask James, he can give you all their addresses."

This was unnecessary, Celia had the addresses already in her notebook. Her next step was to inspect all the addresses from the outside and eliminate the non-starters. The two spinsters in their seventies could be dismissed at once, as Elm Grove consisted of one-bedroom bungalows for the elderly. The garage mechanic's three-bedroom council house was firmly shut up, and a fierce dog snarling through the letter box suggested that everyone was out at work. His son and daughter-in-law seemed to be uncontrollably fertile, to judge from a washing line crammed with children's clothes, three dirty little children playing in the front garden, and shrieks from an angry baby within, all of which left no room to house a mad aunt.

She decided to try the Ickfield Stores first, on the principle that those needing information in a village should apply at the village shop. It was the first real possibility she had seen, with living quarters above and behind it which looked roomy enough to act as an informal prison. But James Hurcomb, presiding from behind his counter over a tempting array of cheeses, was pink, plump and too jolly-looking to make a credible gaoler.

"I wonder if you can help me?" she began. "I believe Joan Berridge is staying with relations in the village, and I'm anxious to get in touch with her."

He treated her to a fat man's happy twinkle. "I'm a relation of hers, second cousin, and she's not staying with me."

"I see. Where else could I ask?"

"Try Rose Villa, three doors up on the other side. Her auntie lives there, she may know."

Out in the street, Celia decided that ninety-year-old Mrs. Hurcomb was disqualified from being thirty-five-year-old Joan Berridge's aunt. The aunt, therefore, was Mrs. Bishop. Was she the aunt who, according to Mrs. Wilson, had "gone to the bad"?

Rose Villa proved to be small and Victorian, with lace curtains over its bay window. Jammed between two older houses in the middle of the High Street, it looked as if it had escaped from some shabby-genteel London suburb dating from the middle of the nineteenth century. It was easy to imagine Joan Berridge cooped up here under the brutal eye of a divorced aunt who had been a nurse before she went to the bad.

The door was answered by a tall, bony woman in her sixties, with a dead white face and improbably black hair. Celia recognised her at once. She had been there among the relatives when Celia paid her visit of condolence to Joan Berridge, and had removed Joan when she started to speak out of turn.

"I believe Joan Berridge is staying here," Celia declared boldly. "And I'd like a word with her."

The pencilled eyebrows shot up in surprise. "My niece Joan? No, I haven't seen her for over a week. What gave you that idea?"

"I'm from Melbury. Someone there thought she'd almost certainly be here."

"Oh?" said Mrs. Bishop. "I wonder why?"

"She left there very suddenly without leaving an address. I think because she was upset about her husband's death. Can you suggest anywhere else she might be?"

"No. I'm sorry, I can't help you."

"At her parents', perhaps?"

The white face twisted into a faint grin. "No."

Deadlock.

"You must excuse me, I've got something on the stove," said Mrs. Bishop, and shut the door in Celia's face.

Walking back despondently to her car, which she had parked outside the church, Celia suddenly felt giddy. At first she attributed this to psychosomatic despair. But on thinking it over further, she decided that as it was ten past five and she had eaten nothing since her sparse breakfast, she was probably faint from hunger. The pub proved to be shut, so she turned and walked back to Ickfield Stores in search of something she could nibble in the car to relieve the pangs. Once there, she realised that she had nothing much at home to make an evening meal with. Moreover she lacked various groceries, which had better be bought now because Englefields in Melbury would be shut long before she got back.

Her route back to the car took her past Rose Villa. As she drew level with it, a largish piece of greenery torn from some shrub landed at her feet, apparently thrown from above. She looked up at the bedroom windows. They were shut, but the lace curtain behind one of them was moving faintly and she heard a sash slam shut.

The piece of greenery still lay at her feet. It was a piece of rosemary, with a snaggy break where it had been torn hastily from the bush.

Rosemary was for remembrance, but that made no sense.

But it also had its French-derived meaning: "Your presence revives me."

Joan Berridge was at Rose Villa. And she wanted to be rescued.

❧ NINE ❧

Celia retired to her car to fortify herself with biscuits and decide on the next step. She had not reacted openly to the piece of rosemary, in case Mrs. Bishop was watching from the window of Rose Villa as well as Joan Berridge. But was anything to be gained by pretending she did not know Joan was there, and going back to Melbury to make plans? No, she could imagine how Ferris would react if she asked for police action to remove an allegedly feeble-minded person from the care of her relatives. Stevens was too wimpish and proper to take part in a forcible rescue, and Bill was not available. Anything that could be done might as well be attempted at once.

She rang the bell again. Mrs. Bishop reappeared, looking even grimmer than before, and opened her mouth to say something which promised to be unpleasant. But Celia got in first. "I know Joan Berridge is here, and I want to see her," she said, and pushed her way into the house.

"How dare you come barging in? I told you. I've no idea where she is."

Celia tried to dodge past her in the narrow hall, but Mrs. Bishop was too large and too strong for her. "Get out of here before I call the police."

"Joan, are you there?" Celia shouted.

They struggled. Celia had managed to kick the front door shut behind her, thus making it difficult to throw her out.

A figure in white had appeared at the far end of the hall, uttering pathetic little moans. It was Joan Berridge, wearing what looked like a nightdress.

Mrs. Bishop abandoned her attempt to throw Celia out, and approached Joan. "Go back to your room, dear," she said in a voice of synthetic honey, "and I'll come and see to you in a minute."

"No! I won't!" Joan cried, and advanced towards Celia eagerly.

Mrs. Bishop seized her roughly by the arm, bundled her into one of the rooms off the hall, and locked her in. Then she turned to Celia and switched back to the honeyed approach. "I'm sorry I told you an untruth when you called earlier. We thought it would be better, in her own interest, that no one from Melbury should see her in this state."

"Really? What state is she in?"

"Not good, I'm afraid. Her mother's been in a home for years, and the shock of her husband's death is threatening to send Joan down the same road. We hope she'll recover with complete peace and quiet, but it's touch and go."

"What nonsense, you sound like the wicked nurse in a ridiculous horror film. She's perfectly sane and wants to go home, let me talk to her."

All traces of honey vanished in a flash. "You're Mrs. Grant, aren't you, her employer. I recognised you at once. You're largely responsible for her condition, fancy sacking her at a moment's notice before her husband was cold in his grave."

"I didn't sack her, she resigned." Celia protested.

"That's not what she says, she's very bitter about it, hysterical in fact. Are you going to leave quietly, or shall I call the police?"

Celia smiled. "Calling the police sounds an excellent idea to me."

This was received in baffled silence.

"Phone them, why don't you?" Celia suggested.

Suddenly Mrs. Bishop became a whirlwind of aggression, seizing Celia by the shoulders and banging her head against the wall of the passage. She flung open the front door and threw Celia out, so violently that she stumbled and fell full length on the pavement. By the time she had picked herself up, the door was shut.

For the present there was nothing more she could do. So she drove home, and spent a miserable evening of drudgery, catching up with urgent paperwork from the nursery in a baffled rage. The village, Colonel Templewood, the Bradshaws and the Hammonds were all ranged against her. With Bill not available, storming Rose Villa and rescuing Joan Berridge was not on, for there was no other muscular young male she could turn to in his place. Her son in the Foreign Office was too respectable, and anyway he was in Washington. She would willingly have hired some bully-boys from the criminal underworld, but how did one get in touch with them?

She went to bed, but was too exhausted to sleep. In the small hours she dozed off uneasily, but soon found herself involved in a repeat of her standard nightmare. But this time, instead of being a pot-bound saxifrage, she was a large, well-established rosemary bush with its roots twisted together painfully in a too-small plastic container. She had managed somehow to ring a bell to draw attention to this state of affairs but no one did anything about it. Slowly drifting into miserable consciousness, she realised that although the plastic container was part of the nightmare, the bell was real. It belonged to her bedside telephone, and the alarm clock showed three in the morning.

"Hello? Who's there?"

The reply came in a faint whisper. "Mrs. Grant? It's Joan. Joan Berridge. I managed not to take the sleeping pill, and I got down to the telephone."

"Good. Tell me what I can do."

"They're sending me on a coach tour. Auntie's taking me. I don't want to go."

"What sort of a coach tour?"

"The West Country, for a fortnight. It starts tomorrow."

Clever, Celia thought. What could be more appropriate than a coach tour, to cheer up a recent widow? She would be even more out of reach than at Rose Villa, for a perfectly respectable reason.

"It's supposed to be a great treat," Joan added in a weepy undertone. "But I want to go home. I'm worried about my plants, after leaving them for so long."

"They're all right, but never mind that now. Where does the coach leave from?"

"The bus station in Welstead. At eight o'clock tomorrow morning."

"And how are you getting to Welstead?"

"Auntie's ordered the village taxi."

Celia thought rapidly. "Have you told your aunt you don't want to go on this trip?"

"Oh no, Mrs. Grant. I'd be afraid to, you don't know what she's like. Ought I to say something?"

"No, for heaven's sake don't. Now listen carefully. There's a ladies by the bus station, between it and the main road. I shall be parked near it in the road. When you get to the bus station, say you have to spend a penny before you get in the coach. Walk past the ladies into the road, and get into the car."

"Oh Mrs. Grant, thank you."

"You remember what my car looks like?"

"Oh dear. I think so, Mrs. Grant."

"Anyway, you'll see me sitting in it. Get in as quickly as you can, and we'll drive away before your aunt can catch up with us. Now have you got all that?"

"Oh yes, Mrs. Grant. I think so."

Celia made her repeat it, and reminded her of the colour and make of the car for good measure. When she had made the arrangements as foolproof as possible, she sent Joan back to bed, set her alarm clock for six and let herself fall into a fitful doze, from which she woke at intervals thinking of all the things that might go horribly wrong.

Not knowing how early the Ickfield taxi would arrive at

169

the bus station, she reached there herself shortly after seven to lie in wait for it, and immediately struck a snag. A huge truck and trailer with French markings had parked itself along the kerb beside the toilet block, in exactly the place where Joan would expect to find her. There was room further along the street, but Joan, in addition to her other disabilities, was far too short-sighted to pick out the right car if it was more than twenty yards away. The only alternative tactic she could think of involved risks, but it would have to do.

Private cars and cabs were driving into the bus station, to drop intending passengers. Parked on the corner where they turned in, Celia kept a sharp look-out for Joan and Mrs. Bishop in the Ickfield taxi. It was twenty to eight, and still they did not come. Had Joan been detected making her phone call? Or was Mrs. Bishop cutting it fine, to give Joan no time to make an escape bid?

That was probably the explanation, for it was almost ten minutes to eight when a taxi containing Joan looking white with panic and Mrs. Bishop looking murderous in a hat turned into the bus station. Celia thrust forward brutally in front of a queue of cars waiting to follow it, and halted behind their taxi at the setting-down point. Mrs. Bishop and Joan got out of the taxi on opposite sides, and the mop-haired young driver began pulling luggage from the boot.

"Here I am, Joan, quick!" said Celia, clutching her arm.

Joan stood stock still with her mouth open, unable to cope with the unexpected. Mrs. Bishop, on the other side of the taxi, was preoccupied with paying the driver and had not yet taken alarm.

Celia tried to pull Joan towards the car, but she resisted. "My suitcase," she moaned.

Celia seized one of the suitcases from the driver. "No, that's Auntie's," Joan protested.

Cursing, Celia grasped the other case and pushed Joan into the passenger seat with the case on top of her. By now Mrs. Bishop was on the rampage. Rushing round from the far side of the taxi, she tried to drag Joan out on to the pavement. But the suitcase, wedged across the door, frustrated her. Rather than join in an unequal battle, Celia got in and drove off in some disarray, with the passenger door open, the suitcase half out of it, and Mrs. Bishop running alongside making little snatches at Joan and screaming abuse.

Joan was whimpering with surprise and fright. "Get that door shut, for heaven's sake," Celia snapped as Mrs. Bishop fell behind at last.

Still clutching the suitcase which had almost been their undoing, Joan managed somehow to get it shut.

"That's right, now push the little button down and lock it."

It was a wise precaution. At the exit from the bus station Celia had to pause to let traffic pass in the main road, and realised that the battle was not yet over. Mrs. Bishop had caught up with them on foot and was trying to open the locked door. When rapping furiously on the window yielded no results, she looked round and saw that the taxi with the mop-haired young driver was next in the queue of cars waiting to leave the bus station. Uttering a few terse words of command, she climbed in, and sat fuming in the passenger seat beside him as she waited to give chase.

Alarmed, Celia caused drivers on the main road to stamp on their brakes and flash their lights angrily as she shot out into the morning rush-hour traffic. But the mop-haired youth, urged on by Mrs. Bishop, followed her through the gap she had created and tried unsuccessfully to pass her and force her to stop. At the next red light he was right behind her. There was no question of shaking him off in a high-speed car chase, for the commuter traffic was heavy and they crawled along in convoy through three more sets of traffic lights. The next one turned red as Celia came up to it. Greatly daring, she played chicken last across, but proved to be the last chicken but one. A welcome sound of clashing headlamps behind her announced that she was the last to make the crossing unscathed. Back at the intersection, the usual shouts of reproach broke out. The taxi was slewed across the road and the mop-haired youth was getting out. The pursuit was at an end.

Once clear of the town, she paused to reorganise. Joan Berridge was still twittering with nerves, but let Celia relieve her of the suitcase on her lap and do up her seat belt. As they drove on she was still uttering little moaning exclamations in which gratitude to Celia was mixed with horror at what she had just been through and condemnations of Auntie. "She's horrid, I've always hated her. And wicked. She was put in prison once because of something she'd done."

"Really? What sort of thing?" Celia asked.

"Something about drugs and an old lady she was looking after. I never heard the rights and the wrongs of it, but it must have been very bad because she had to stop being a nurse. So she went back home to look after Grandad and Grandma, and all my cousins were cross about that because they say she's after Grandad and Grandma's money."

Coffee and rolls at a wayside inn had a calming effect on Joan, and Celia began to debrief her. "Joan, how did you come to be staying with your aunt?"

"Uncle George took me there, and told her to shut me away. He knew she was a bad woman, there'd been a lot of talk in the family about her and how she was always after money."

Quite, Celia thought. The only question was, how much had George Tunney paid her for her services. "Why did he want you shut away?" she asked.

"Because I'd changed my mind," said Joan, showing signs of distress.

"About what you'd told the police?"

"Oh dear me, that's right, Mrs. Grant. I'm sorry about all those things I said about Mr. Wilkins, but my head was all in a muddle then, and I let Uncle George over-persuade me. I wouldn't have told all those lies if I hadn't been cross with Mr. Wilkins over something that happened. I thought . . . well, I thought he'd been rude to me, but I deserved it, I see that now. Mr. Wilkins was quite right, it was my own silly fault. And then when Mr. Wilkins was arrested I felt awful, because by then the muddle in my head had stopped, and I saw what Uncle George had been up to."

Encouraged by these introductory remarks, Celia made her start her story at the beginning, with the events on the evening of Simon's death.

"I always worried when Berridge went out for the evening," Joan began. "I used to watch out for him when it got to closing time, so I'd know what mood he was in and whether he'd want something to eat, and if he was very late I'd worry, for fear of him not finding his way home. So I was looking out through the curtains as usual, and I heard a noise and there was Mr. Wilkins, standing there in the front garden, and I thought, that's funny, what's he doing there?"

"One moment, Joan. What time was this?"

"Oh, just coming up to closing time, I reckon. I waited a bit and Berridge still hadn't come home, and when I looked out next Mr. Wilkins had gone."

Closing time at the Red Lion was ten thirty. If Bill had left soon after she saw him, his alibi was intact.

"Then a bit later," Joan went on, "I heard Berridge coming down the road, singing the way he sometimes does when he's had a few. So I looked out again, and there was Uncle George coming up behind him, shouting something. But Berridge was in one of his bad moods, he kept turning round and cursing at Uncle George—"

"Did you hear what they were saying?" Celia asked.

"Oh no, they were too far away. And in the end Uncle George took hold of Berridge's arm and turned him round and they went away together. And I thought, oh good, he's taking Berridge back to his place to cool off a bit before he comes home. He's nice that way, Uncle George is."

So he used to knock her about when he came home drunk, Celia thought, and that is the nearest she can get to admitting as much to a stranger. Aloud, she said, "Can you remember roughly what time this was?"

"Quite soon after I looked out and saw that Mr. Wilkins wasn't there any more."

"And that was the last you saw of your husband?"

"That's right, and in the morning he hadn't been home and I thought, well, he must have fallen asleep round there. So on my way to work I called in there, and Uncle George said, no, he's not here. And I said, that's funny, he was with you last thing last night, I saw you. And Uncle George said, yes, he'd had a few and I tried to get him to come round here for a bit, but he got difficult and halfway along he turned round to go home. And then I was really worried, Mrs. Grant, because Berridge has a weak chest and last time he slept out under a hedge I had him in bed for a fortnight. So I waited in all day for him to come home, but he never did."

Unbelievably, she was shedding tears for a man who had treated her like a doormat.

When she had recovered, she went on to explain what had happened when the police reported that her husband had not been drowned accidentally. "Uncle George came round and said, better not tell the police about seeing me with your Simon that night, it might give them wrong ideas, and anyway I know who killed him, it was that Wilkins. And he told me how Mr. Wilkins had quarrelled with Berridge in the Red Lion and then gone out looking for him to knock him about some more. And I said, that's funny, Mr. Wilkins was here looking for Berridge just before you and he came along. And Uncle George said, there you are, it just goes to show. And then he thought for a bit and said, look Joanie, you don't want your old uncle to be asked a lot of questions when he was only doing you a good turn, keeping Berridge out of your way till he'd sobered up. So don't say you saw me, and anyway we know who did it, so how about making the story a bit more convincing-like? Well, I was angry with Mr. Wilkins and Uncle George kept on at me, saying how we village people should stick together against the incomers and not let one of us be blamed for something one of them had done. He went on and on about it, and in the end he persuaded me and I let him tell me what to say to the police."

"So when you said you saw Bill Wilkins chasing your husband down the road, it wasn't true?"

"That's right, Mrs. Grant, and I feel awful about it, I could cut out my tongue, I really could. Because after a bit I got thinking. Why's Uncle George so keen for me to tell all those lies? I thought. And after a bit I worked it out. He'd killed Berridge himself."

This burst of intellect astonished Celia. "Really? Why did he do that?"

"To keep Berridge quiet. Years ago Uncle George did something very bad, and when the Bradshaws came to live here Berridge had been saying he'd tell everyone about it unless he got some money."

"D'you know what it was your uncle did?" Celia asked, trying to keep the eagerness out of her voice.

"Yes, Mrs. Grant. Berridge told me. But it's not very nice, I'd rather not say."

"I think I know, Joan. Was it about who was the father of your sister-in-law Barbara's baby?"

Her eyes opened wide. "Oh Mrs. Grant, how did you find out?"

Roger Stevens took another look at the affidavit that Joan Berridge had just sworn to. "I really do congratulate you, Mrs. Grant. I shall tell the partners that when next we need a private enquiry agent, we couldn't do better than ask you."

"Horrors no, I've my hands full running the nursery. Any more last straws, and the camel's back will be a mass of slipped discs."

He frowned at the affidavit. "There are some good points for the defence in this. We've evidence now that Tunney was the last person to have seen the victim alive, that he bullied Mrs. Berridge into making false statements which incriminated another person, and that he had her abducted when she insisted on telling the truth. We also now have evidence of Tunney's motive for the killing: Berridge was threatening to make public Tunney's incestuous relationship with his niece. But we're not out of the wood yet. Counsel for the prosecution will challenge our key witnesses. They'll make the most of Mrs. Berridge's alleged mental instability, and the fact that she's changed her evidence weakens it. The Tidmarshes will be given a rough time for changing their evidence on the question of Mr. Wilkins' alibi. It's not an open and shut case.''

"But you keep talking about what would happen at the trial. Surely we can use the committal proceedings to show that there's no case to answer?"

He thought for a moment. "We could produce the evidence in court next week. At the very least the magistrate would have to remand our client for further police enquiries.''

No, Celia thought. Bill had been rotting in his cell for quite long enough. And she had no faith in police enquiries by the obnoxious Ferris.

"We could try for bail," Stevens added. "Magistrates usually grant it if there's obviously a serious doubt about the defendant's guilt.''

Better, she thought, but not good enough. Bill released, with a murder charge still hanging over him, would be an impossible psychological handful, convinced that the whole of Melbury was "pointing at him." She had realised long ago that Stevens was a legalistic wimp, and knew she would have to take the law into her own hands. She had already worked out what seemed to her a foolproof plan.

"I'll send Ferris a copy of this," Stevens was saying as he picked up Joan's affidavit.

"No, don't. Not yet, there's still five days to go, and there's a dodge I want to try first. Make me twelve copies of it on your machine, and put the original in your safe.''

"Really? Why, Mrs. Grant? What are you proposing to do?"

"Something you wouldn't approve of, so I shan't tell you about it. Get along with you and have those photocopies made.''

Joan was sitting on a hard chair in the outer office, looking worried. "Oh Mrs. Grant, I've been thinking," she began. "I wish I could go home now but I can't, it's not safe. I'd be in hot water with Uncle George, he'd try to shut me up again."

Celia, who had been nerving herself to point this out to her, was grateful for this fitful gleam of common sense. "I've been thinking the same thing. How would you like a little holiday in a hotel in, say, Brighton?"

"Oh no, Mrs. Grant, I couldn't stay in a hotel, I never have. I could go to my sister's in Tonbridge, she and her husband have a flower shop there."

"Does George Tunney know about your sister?"

"Oh dear, perhaps he does."

"Your aunt Edna does anyway, she'd tell him. We daren't risk it."

The threat of a hotel made her hysterical, but where else could she go? It was a maddening problem. With so much to do and only five days to do it, Celia grudged every minute she had to spend on it. After various friends and acquaintances had produced urgent reasons for not giving Joan asylum, she rang her Uncle Hugo in desperation, and made him square his housekeeper of whom he was terrified, and agree to take her in.

"But you say she's half-witted," he said nervously. "How do I keep her amused?"

"Give her a sick plant to nurse back to health, and she'll settle down quite contentedly, you'll find. There's a monstera in a terminal state of neglect in your front hall, just show her that and she'll give you no trouble."

Having sent Joan off, clucking like an alarmed hen, in a hire car, she went back to her office, where a message was waiting for her: could she ring Ted Bradshaw as soon as she got in? She did, and found that he wanted to talk to her urgently. She was equally keen to talk to him, but away from the interruptions of the office. So she arranged for him to come to her house for a drink before lunch.

She was clearing her desk of nursery business when Peter Verney thrust his head round the office door. "Thought about what I said yesterday, Celia?"

"Why should I bother to think about your sordid career of greed?"

"That's not a very wise attitude. I've told Ferris I may have important evidence to give him."

"Your 'important evidence' would get you charged with perjury if the case ever came to court, but it won't."

"That's not what Ferris says."

"Ferris is in a state of happy ignorance about recent developments, and so are you. Get out now, I'm busy."

He reached for her handbag and opened it. "Let's have a bit more on account while we talk things over."

"Put that down or I shall call the police."

He paused, with the handbag still open.

"I mean it, Peter," she said.

"No you don't."

Celia rang Welstead central police station. "Detective-Inspector Ferris, please."

He was out, it seemed.

"Then can I leave a message? It's Mrs. Grant of Archerscroft Nurseries. Could he ring back? I want to report a case of attempted blackmail."

Peter Verney dropped the handbag hastily. "Right, Celia," he shouted in a fury. "You've asked for it and you're going to get it."

"Slither away into the undergrowth, you silly little rattlesnake, and don't come back."

This time he went, and she hurried back to her house to find Ted Bradshaw walking up the path in front of her to keep their drinks date.

"Barbara asked me to come," he said when she had settled him down with a beer. "She's worried sick. There's a nasty bit of past history that she's very ashamed of. You've found out about it somehow, and you're trying to prove a connection between it and her brother's murder."

"I'm not trying to prove it, I've succeeded. You'd better read this."

She handed him a copy of Joan Berridge's sworn statement. He glanced down it, said "Good God!," then settled down to a concentrated read. When he had finished, he gave it back to her. "Have you handed this to the police?"

"Not yet."

"I suppose you realise that the publicity will shatter her?"

"Yes, but I've got a plan. If everyone behaves sensibly, there'll be no need to make it public."

"I don't understand."

"I shall invite Tunney to go to the police and confess. But he won't give his true reason for killing Simon. He'll say they quarrelled over something quite different, and he hit Simon a bit too hard, panicked and dumped him in the river."

"Okay if it works. But why would he agree?"

"Because the alternative is to be exposed in court as a child abuser."

"He could still deny that and try to brazen it out."

"If he does, we can put him under a lot of pressure from other people who don't want this story told in public. You and Barbara, for instance. You could make it clear unofficially that unless and until Tunney has given himself up to the police, no member or connection by marriage of the Tunney or Berridge families will be considered for employment at the mill. Colonel Templewood's determined that the past should stay buried, with any luck he'll threaten to cut off all future benefactions to the village unless Tunney agrees to go quietly. Then there are a lot of village worthies whose faces will be very red if it comes out that they blackmailed Paul Templewood and let your Barbara take the blame. With all these people yelling at George Tunney, and the threat of exposure as a child abuser hanging over him, he'll decide that he'd rather do what he's told and go gracefully to prison for manslaughter."

Suddenly Bradshaw was trying not to laugh.

"What's so funny?" Celia asked crossly.

"You look like a china doll and you behave like a Colombian drug baron on the rampage."

"In this sort of situation one has to. Does Barbara talk to you freely about what happened?"

"Not at all, if she can help it."

"Oh dear. She wouldn't talk to me, so could you try to get some answers from her?"

"I can try. What are the questions?"

"When I'm putting the screws on, it would be helpful to know who knew what at what stage. For instance, at what stage did George Tunney find out about the teenagers' blackmail conspiracy? Does Colonel Templewood know the truth? Did Ron Tunney know before the inquest that Barbara was going to say Paul was the child's father?"

"I think her brother Simon did. That's the bit of the nightmare that rankles most. The looked-up-to elder brother kept his mouth shut and let her be crucified as a blackmailer. Anyway I'll find out what I can and let you know."

When he had gone she cooked herself an omelette, then wrote a hasty note to Bill. She would come and see him if possible, but was very busy organising his release, which would happen at the committal proceedings if not before, as he would see from the copy, which she enclosed, of Joan Berridge's sworn statement.

The doorbell rang as she was licking the envelope shut. Barbara Bradshaw stood outside, looking pale and tragic. "May I come in?"

"Of course."

"Ted said I'd feel better if I talked to you about it, and I think I shall."

After agitated apologies for her cold treatment of Celia, she fell silent, wringing her hands. "Oh dear, I don't know where to begin."

"Why not at the beginning? When did the thing start?"

Another long silence. "When I was about nine, I suppose."

"Tell me about it."

"He used to come up to my room to say goodnight to

180

me, that's what he called it. And when I asked him not to, he said I was only a niece and he'd turn me out of the house if I told Aunt Kathleen. I wouldn't have told her anyway, he'd somehow made me feel I was the guilty one with the dirty secret. But Aunt Kathleen knew what was happening and didn't interfere, I worked that out later and I've never forgiven her for it. She wouldn't let Dick or Simon come upstairs while Uncle George was 'saying goodnight' to me.''

She was speaking less hesitantly now, as she warmed to her story.

"And then, when I was fifteen, there was going to be the baby.'' She paused. "He was in a panic and made me try all sorts of things to get rid of it, because he was afraid people would guess about him and me. And then Paul killed himself and Uncle George said why didn't I say Paul was the father, because he was dead and couldn't contradict. So I agreed, because in a queer way I was quite fond of Uncle George, and by then I knew that what we'd been doing was really wicked, much worse than going with a boy, and I didn't want him to get into trouble. And when the police came round I said my piece as we'd agreed. The policeman asked me if I'd had any money off Paul, and I said no and didn't think any more about it. Then at the inquest it all came out about how Paul had been stealing to raise money and everyone decided that I must have been blackmailing him, and making him miserable, and I was the cause of that awful tragedy.''

"Oh, poor you. How soon did you find out who the real blackmailers were?"

Barbara thought for a moment. "I'd realised vaguely for some time that Dick and Simon were suddenly able to afford airguns and things like that that they wanted, but I didn't know why. And then after the inquest I think Uncle George must have got a hint from somewhere, and he had Dick and Simon on the carpet and there were a lot of angry voices behind closed doors, and I kept asking what was going on, and no one would tell me. In the end I went to Aunt Kathleen and said if I wasn't told I'd go to the police and say Uncle George was the baby's father. And Aunt Kathleen said I was a slut and I'd led Uncle George on, and then she called him in and he went all panicky and fierce, shouting that I was a wicked ungrateful girl and so on. In the end I agreed not to go to the police if they told me what was going on."

"And when they told you, you realised how badly Simon had let you down."

"That was the worst moment of all. He knew perfectly well whose baby it was, and he kept quiet and let me tell that story about Paul at the inquest. So did Ron, but it was Simon letting me walk into that trap that really hurt. He was my elder brother and up till then he'd always stood up for me in the family. Afterwards I hated him, I couldn't even keep my food down if he was at the table. So in the end I decided that if I let everyone go on thinking Paul was the baby's father, Colonel Templewood would pay for me to have it somewhere else, and I need never come back to Melbury."

"Did Colonel Templewood ever find out the truth?"

"No, but someone had told him I was an easy lay and all the boys had had me, but I'd fixed on Paul because I could get money out of him. And after about a month he came to the place in Birmingham where Dr. Hammond had arranged for me to stay, and he was horrible to me. I was a wicked girl, he said, and he'd go on paying for me till I'd had the baby, but only because he'd promised to, and he hoped I'd never have the nerve to show my face in Melbury again, and he wouldn't do a thing for me or the baby once I'd had it and was able to earn."

"What happened to the baby?" Celia asked.

"It was stillborn. I managed to see Doctor Hammond once without Aunt Kathleen and told him the truth and asked him if it would be deformed or mad, and he said it wouldn't. Of course I didn't believe that and I was glad it died. But it's wicked to wish your child dead, isn't it?"

"I think you should forgive yourself. Don't go on punishing yourself, you're punishing Ted as well."

"I know. Till I realised that we were coming back here I'd buried it deep down, I'd almost forgotten about it. It was the thought of having to face my horrible family again that brought it back. Ted says you're going to manage so that nothing will come out publicly, can you really?"

"I hope so, barring accidents."

Barbara shivered. "So do I. There are some questions you want to ask me, Ted says. What are they?"

"You've answered them already."

"Oh, good. You will be able to keep this horrible story hushed up?"

Celia repeated her assurance with more conviction than she felt. Barbara lunged at her clumsily and gave her a great hug, then dashed off home with her eyes full of tears.

Early in the afternoon Detective-Inspector Ferris returned her phone call. "Mrs. Grant? You rang me this morning while I was out. What's all this about you being blackmailed?"

"Oh, it was only someone who was threatening to give false evidence against Mr. Wilkins unless I handed over some money. It will be quite easy to prove that he's lying, but I thought I might as well give him a bit of a fright."

"Is this your neighbour Dr. Verney? He's been in touch with me, and I must warn you formally. Trying to frighten witnesses is liable to land you in court."

"Mr. Verney's the one who'll land in court, for perjury. That is, if the case comes to court and you take any notice of his nonsense."

"Another thing. Your solicitor's been in touch with me, the Tidmarshes have changed their story. This is another of your tricks, what d'you mean by interfering with my witnesses."

"What d'you mean by pressurising 'your' witnesses into telling lies?"

"You're a mischief-maker and a threat to the administration of justice, Mrs. Grant."

"And you, Inspector Ferris, are so grotesque that no one

would hire you as a minor police character in a second-rate crime series on television."

He slammed down the phone in a fury, and Celia reproached herself for unwise and unladylike behaviour. Even under stress, one should not say things like that to the police.

When she had recovered her temper after this interruption, she drove to Colonel Templewood's to persuade him to play his part in putting pressure on George Tunney. The nightmare-gothic mansion was looking as desolate and neglected as ever. The sinister Burchett answered the door, and looked doubtful when she asked to see the colonel.

"But I must, it's very important."

"Is it about what you were on about the other day? If it is, he won't see you."

"Say I want his help to prevent a sordid scandal in the village."

He studied her thoughtfully for a moment. There had been a change in him. He no longer called her "madam," and whether she saw the colonel or not seemed to be for him to decide.

"A sordid eighteen-year-old scandal?" he asked.

"Yes."

"Then you'd better come inside."

When they stood facing each other in the gloomy, echoing hall he said, "Tell me what this is all about, why don't you?"

She stiffened. "I came to talk to the colonel."

This seemed to amuse him. "Very well, come this way."

It was the room she had been shown into on her previous visit. The colonel was already there, but he was not the fine figure of an old soldier whom she remembered from last time. He lay slumped in an armchair half asleep, wearing stained slacks and a cardigan that had come unravelled at the elbows. An unheeded television in a corner dispensed the inane dialogue and guffawing laughter of a sitcom. On a table beside him were an almost empty bottle of whisky, a glass and what looked like the half-eaten remains of his lunch.

"Lady to see you, Colonel," said Burchett loudly to rouse him.

The old man looked blearily at Celia, then made a drink-sodden attempt to rise.

"Please don't get up," she said hastily.

He lurched back into the armchair. "What? . . . What?" he croaked.

Celia began to explain that she had identified Simon Berridge's murderer and penetrated the eighteen-year-old secret, but was hoping to avoid a public scandal in the village.

"What? What? I don't understand . . ." His speech was slurred, and it was clear that he had taken nothing in.

"You see?" said Burchett contemptuously. "This is how it is when he's not going out in the evening."

"Would it be better if I came back tomorrow morning?"

"Not much. Why don't you talk to me, nowadays I often have to act on my own initiative."

She was holding a copy of Joan Berridge's statement which she had intended to show to the colonel. Burchett held out his hand for it. He was very much in charge, the secret power broker behind the colonel's decrepit throne, and he clearly revelled in it. Did he know all about the colonel's failure of nerve in the Normandy beachhead? Probably. She could imagine him taunting the old man with it, to show him who was the real master.

He took Joan Berridge's statement from her and read it. "Ah yes, I was afraid you'd blast the lid off that can of worms. You say you want to avoid a scandal. How?"

Celia explained her plan. "Bradshaw will put pressure on Tunney to confess, and I was hoping the colonel would do the same."

Burchett produced a death's-head grin. "He would, I'd see to that, if your plan was workable. But it isn't. George Tunney isn't here to be leant on. He's bolted."

♣ TEN ♣

"Bolted?" Celia echoed, horrified.

Burchett nodded. "Kathleen Tunney says he was called away suddenly to the funeral of a cousin in Norfolk. He's the executor, she says, and she doesn't know when he'll be back."

"When did he go?" she asked.

"Yesterday morning."

A whole day before Joan Berridge's escape from Mrs. Bishop. Had something else frightened him into bolting? Or was the deceased cousin in Norfolk genuine? Perhaps Burchett knew.

"I never heard him mention one," he told her.

Celia was in despair. If Tunney had fled rather than face the music, a disastrous new scenario opened up. She would have to break faith with Barbara and blow the ancient scandal wide open next week in court. The whole village, led by the Hammonds, would reproach her for stirring up unwanted mud. All the guilty parties would deny their guilt, Ferris would accuse her of interfering with prosecution witnesses, and whether this would help get Bill freed was an open question. But she could see no alternative.

Burchett reacted violently when she told him her intentions. "Oh, no you don't. You can't do that to the colonel. Look at him."

Celia had been aware for some time of hoarse, throat-clearing noises behind her. She turned, and saw her mistake. The colonel had picked up Barbara Berridge's statement and grasped its gist. His face had crumpled into misery like a child's. The sounds she had heard were of harsh male weeping.

"Look at him," Burchett repeated. "It's haunted him ever since, if you bring it all up again you'll kill him."

"I'm sorry. The village has kept quiet while an innocent man was charged with a murder they know he didn't commit. They'll have to take the consequences unless Tunney can be found and made to produce his heavily censored confession."

"Give me a few days before you do anything. Maybe he does have a cousin in Norfolk."

"Who's chosen this convenient moment to die? No. It's too much of a coincidence to be believable."

"Wait, can't you, in case he turns up."

"There's no time, the court hearing's on Tuesday."

Burchett's beady eyes narrowed with venom. "If you land us all in the bloody cart with your nonsense, we'll make the village too hot for you."

"You must be out of your mind," said Celia coldly, and marched from the room.

Burchett came hurrying after her. "Mrs. Grant, wait."

But Celia would not wait, and ignored him when he followed her out to her car. He was probably right, the village could make life difficult for her if she persisted, but what else could she do?

She had been back at Archerscroft less than five minutes when Ann Hammond rang. "Burchett's been on to me, Celia. You can't do this."

"Oh yes I can, and will. It's time someone did a bit of plain speaking, there's too much hypocrisy in this village."

"What's wrong with hypocrisy? Where would we be without white lies? At each other's throats the whole damn time. You'll never be forgiven, Celia. I'll hold it against you, so will a lot of others. The village won't like it. You'll have trouble getting staff."

"If the village chooses to behave like Sodom and Gomorrah, it must take the consequences. Please get off the line, Ann. I want to ring my solicitor about the court proceedings on Tuesday."

She was lucky, Stevens was in his office. "The dodge I'd thought of hasn't worked," she told him. "So could you send a copy of Joan Berridge's affidavit to Ferris straight away?"

He hesitated. "If we do, he'll have lots of time to prepare evidence to the effect that Mrs. Berridge is mentally unstable and not to be relied on. It would be better to let it come to him as a surprise in court."

"Very well, let's do it that way. Will they release Bill?"

"It depends entirely on how the magistrate reacts."

She fretted over this for the rest of the afternoon. That night in bed she had nightmares about Bill getting tied up in knots by prosecuting counsel and losing his temper, Barbara cursing her and denying that her uncle had ever touched her, Ann Hammond urging the village to raze Archerscroft to the ground. Despair had got the upper hand, and she was astonished, when answering a breakfast time ring at the door, to find, not the postman with something for her to sign, but the tall grey-headed figure of George Tunney, haggard in the morning sunlight.

He pushed his way roughly past her into the house. "Where is she? What have you done with her?"

"Ah, I'm glad you've come," she said as calmly as possible. "Do sit down, you and I need to talk."

"I'll do the talking, missis. Where's Joan?"

"Out of harm's way. I've a proposition to put to you—"

He seized her shoulders and shook her roughly. "I don't want to hear no propositions, I want my niece back."

"Then this isn't the way to go about it. Let go of me please."

188

He released her unwillingly. "What's she told you? She's mental, she's not responsible for what she says. Have you been putting words in her mouth?"

It would be dangerous, Celia decided, to tell him about Joan's affidavit till she had calmed him down. "Mr. Tunney, you look all in. Let's sit down and discuss this sensibly. I'm sure some coffee would do you good, I'll get you some."

She set off towards the kitchen, but he followed close behind her. As she passed the telephone in the hall he gripped her from behind, pinning her arms to her sides. "Oh, no you don't."

"I wasn't thinking of phoning anyone."

"You better not." He half dragged, half carried her back into the living room and dumped her on the sofa. "You and I are staying here till you tell me where she is."

"If you knew, it wouldn't do you any good. She's made her statement already, and it's in a safe place."

"Lies. She's a no-good liar and a cheat, just like her husband."

Celia saw no point in arguing. Silence fell. The postman's footsteps came up the path. Tunney gripped her again and put a rough hand over her mouth to silence her. Letters fell through the slot into the hall and the footsteps went away again.

"Let's go into the kitchen, shall we?" she suggested when he released her. "I was just having breakfast, I'm sure you could do with some too."

But this attempt to establish a normal atmosphere had the opposite effect. In a sudden burst of rage he hit her hard across the face, twice, and began shouting abuse. How dare she abduct Joan and disrupt the family's plans for her? He had paid for the coach tour as a treat, to take her mind off her bereavement. He would have the law on Celia for interfering, he would drive her out of the village.

The outburst ended, as suddenly as it had begun. Celia was terrified. He was at the end of his tether, totally unpredictable.

He was sitting opposite her, staring at her in perplexity and muttering to himself. From the odd word she was able to catch, the connecting thread seemed to be Joan's dishonesty, mental confusion and unreliability as a witness. Would it be safe now, she wondered, to tell him what Joan had said in her statement, and put her proposal to him? Or would it provoke another violent outburst?

Out in the hall, the telephone began to ring.

"Don't answer it," Tunney ordered.

"I must, I know who it is," she lied. "If I don't answer, they'll know there's something wrong."

Greatly daring, she stood up and went to the phone, expecting to be attacked at any moment. Tunney followed her out into the hall, breathing hard down her neck. "No cheating, mind."

The call was from Burchett. "Good news, Mrs. Grant. You won't need to produce that evidence of yours after all. George Tunney got back home late last night."

"I know."

"How? He's not there with you?"

"Yes."

"In a dangerous mood?"

"Yes."

"I'll be with you soon as I can," Burchett promised, and put the phone down.

"That's right, on the ten-thirty train," said Celia for Tunney's benefit. "I'll meet it at Welstead."

Instead of going back to the living room, she went into the kitchen. Tunney followed. She poured a cup of coffee from the filter machine. "Sugar?" she asked, offering it.

Tunney frowned at the coffee cup as if it presented a threat, then surrendered and took it. His eyes moved to the toast on the table. Celia wondered when he had last eaten and drunk.

"I'll make some fresh," she said as he reached for the toast-rack. "That's gone soggy."

"No," he snapped and took a piece, which he smothered in butter and marmalade and ate with fierce concentration.

190

Celia waited on him in tense silence, knowing that anything she said might shatter his fragile calm. Without asking him whether he wanted bacon and eggs she cooked him some. He watched the frying pan suspiciously, as if he feared a trick. When the plateful was ready he ate it, staring at her angrily between mouthfuls.

After two more pieces of toast and marmalade, he stood up. "Time I knocked some sense out of you. Where's Joan?"

"With a relative of mine."

"Where?"

"I'll tell you later if you'll sit down and discuss this thing calmly."

"No, now," he roared, and up-ended the table so that everything on it crashed to the floor.

He rushed at her. She snatched an ultra-sharp kitchen knife from the rack and dodged round the overturned table. He followed, and reached out to grab her wrist and make her drop the knife, but stumbled over one of the table legs and fell headlong. She made for the hall, and reached it in time to slam the kitchen door in his face as he stumbled after her. By the time he got it open again she had darted into the lavatory off the hall and locked herself in.

His footsteps crossed the hall into the living room, then paused and came back. The door-handle rattled violently. "You in there, Mrs. Grant?"

She said nothing, scarcely daring to breathe. He rattled the door again, then crashed his shoulder against it to break it down. But it was solid, and resisted two more assaults. He grunted, and went away. Looking for an axe, probably, to attack the door with.

Should she let herself out while he was away and make a dash for it? As she hesitated, voices made themselves heard out in the hall. Burchett had arrived, and was talking quietly, trying to calm Tunney down. But with little success it seemed, for Tunney was roaring at him.

Presently there was a knock on the door of her retreat. "Are you in there, madam?" asked Burchett's voice.

"Yes."

"If you don't mind staying there for a moment, madam, I'll tell you when it's safe to come out."

He went, and Tunney started bellowing again. A woman had arrived and joined in, bellowing back at Tunney. It sounded like Ann Hammond.

The shouting lasted for what seemed a long time before it died down. Tunney seemed to have fallen silent, and the other two were talking in normal conversational tones. It sounded as if the situation was under control, so she let herself out of the lavatory and walked into the living room. George Tunney was sitting in an armchair. Burchett and Ann Hammond towered over him, like prosecuting counsel. Ann was holding a copy of Joan Berridge's statement.

"Ah hello, Celia," she said. "Come on in."

As if I was late for a meeting, she thought. Should she say, "I'm sorry, I was defending myself with a kitchen knife against a murderous attack"?

"We've propositioned George here," Ann explained, bringing the latecomer up to date, "but we haven't explained to him yet what the consequences will be if he tries to brazen it out. No jobs for Tunneys or Berridges at the mill. Public disgrace for everyone involved in blackmailing Paul Templewood, including his son Ron who's supposed to be a pure and stainless policeman. And the colonel's furious, isn't he, Burchett?"

"That's right, madam, I've never seen him so angry. He says he's not having that old business raked up again, with all the old dirt coming out. If George here doesn't play ball, he'll cut off all the money he gives to the village, stop subsidising the flower show and the old people's club and all the other things, and he'll plough up the cricket field. He's every right to, George, it's on his land. He'll punish the village for what you've done."

Tunney said nothing, but sat staring at his shoes.

"George, this has been a bit of a shock, I realise that," said Ann. "Sleep on it, we'll give you twenty-four hours to make up your mind."

"I'm not confessing to nothing," Tunney shouted suddenly. "It's all lies, what Joan says, she's mental, you've put words in her mouth."

"No, George," Burchett argued. "There are people besides her can prove every word of it's true."

"I'm going, I've heard enough bloody nonsense," Tunney shouted. He rose from his chair, pushed Ann roughly out of his way and strode out of the house, slamming the front door behind him.

"You're letting him go?" Celia queried.

"Don't worry madam," said Burchett calmly. "He's slow at taking things in, but when he has he's quite reasonable. He'll see it our way in the end."

Celia noted with interest that she had become "madam" again, probably to maintain parity with Ann Hammond, who was also "madam." Which of them was the real power broker, Burchett behind his manservant screen, or Ann?

"George will toe the line all right," said Ann, with the air of one closing a satisfactory public meeting, "and Celia can keep all that dirt of hers to herself."

"No," said Celia. "He's criminally insane. I've just been defending myself against him with a kitchen knife. He was proposing to bash me about till I told him where Joan Berridge was."

"Well, you can understand him wanting to find out," said Ann.

"Perhaps, but answer me this. How did he know she wasn't on that coach tour? He left the day before it started and got back late last night. Who would have told him? How would they have got hold of him? He knew because he'd followed the route of the tour, spying on it."

"Oh really, madam, why would he want to follow her around?"

"Because he'd realised that he'd have to kill her to be safe. He was going to organise a fatal 'accident' for her miles away from Melbury. When he found she wasn't on the tour, he phoned the aunt who was supposed to be going with her, and she told him what I'd done."

"Oh dear," said Ann.

"Till an hour ago, I was prepared to give him the benefit of the doubt over Simon's death. I can't now, I'm sure it was cold-blooded murder. If we let him pretend that he killed Simon by accident in the heat of a quarrel, he'll get off with a light sentence or none at all. A murderer who gets away with it once is liable to kill again. Are we prepared to let that happen?"

There was a long pause. Ann and Burchett consulted each other mutely.

"Actually that had occurred to us, madam," said Burchett. "We've taken it into account in our planning, you can leave matters safely in our hands."

"We wouldn't have told you if you hadn't worked it out," said Ann. "We thought you might worry, you're not as tough as we are."

She stared at them. "I don't understand."

"Then you've nothing to worry about, have you?" said Ann.

Suddenly it dawned on her. "Oh no!"

"It's the only clean way out for him," Ann declared. "Better than being dragged through the courts as a murderer and child abuser."

Celia was horrified. "You propose to bully him into killing himself."

"Of course we do, don't be so squeamish. Listen, Celia. If a village is to run smoothly, someone has to take the lead. Poor old Templewood's past it, so now Burchett and I run Melbury between us. There are times when someone has to take responsibility for harsh decisions, and this is one of them."

Celia stared at them in silent horror. They were power-mad monsters, both of them. How dare they treat the village as a private fiefdom, ruled by arbitrary whim? What right had they to sit in life-or-death judgement on a fellow human being?

"You're not worried about what's best for George Tunney," she protested. "All you really care about is suppressing an eighteen-year-old scandal."

"We care about that too, and why not?" Ann stormed. "There's a good spirit in the village now, people pull together. When the mill gets going again we'll have hardly any unemployment, and we've frozen almost all the building land round the village to keep the commuters out. Why should we put all that to risk? Why should Barbara Berridge be put through the mincer all over again? Why should poor old Templewood have his nose rubbed in the fact that his son was a coward? Why should a lot of respectable men in their thirties be pilloried eighteen years after the event over a teenage prank that went wrong? I know how you feel, Celia. We all have gut reactions against things like this, it's understandable. But they can't be helped, so don't worry."

Celia did worry. For the next twenty-four hours she was restless to the point of lunacy, unable to settle down to work at the nursery, unwilling to pay her promised visit to Bill, shut up in a black nightmare. They had made her an accomplice, she was just as guilty as they were. Should she interfere? How? Did she really want George Tunney brought to court and tried? Late that evening Burchett rang her to say that everything was "proceeding according to plan" and would she please make sure that Joan Berridge's affidavit was not handed to the police. "You see, they would have to produce it at the inquest, madam, and that would be most awkward." She went to bed, and woke in a cold sweat from one of the most horrible nightmares she had ever experienced, in which George Tunney was drowning in the mill-race and she stood there paralysed, unable to save him.

She was sitting in her office next morning, pretending to work, when Burchett walked in uninvited. "Here you are, madam. I think this is what you've been wanting."

She took the sheet of paper from its envelope and read:

"Dear Mrs. Grant,

I am writing this to confess to you that I killed my nephew Simon Berridge. That evening in the Red Lion he made an insulting reference to my wife. I ran into him on his way home and he repeated the remark. I hit him and he fell to the ground. When I realised that he was dead, I panicked, and threw him into the river, hoping that it would pass as an accident, owing to him being drunk at the time. I sincerely regret having kept silent and allowing suspicion to fall on Mr. Wilkins, and hope he will forgive me for any inconvenience caused.

Yours truly,
George Tunney.

"Where is he?" Celia asked, fearing the answer.

"There's been a tragedy, madam," said Burchett calmly. "He couldn't fact the disgrace. He's thrown himself under a train at Welstead station."

"I see. When did this happen?"

"An hour ago. I happened to be on the platform at the time."

He was looking completely unmoved. Did he really feel nothing? He and Ann had talked Tunney into it, but she was as responsible as he was, she had known that this was what they intended and she had let them go ahead. Why? Because murderers had to be prevented from causing further harm? Yes, but not by a kangaroo court consisting of the doctor's wife and someone's manservant. Because of the unpopularity she herself would face if Tunney was tried and the true story came out? Perhaps. Because it was the best way out for Tunney? Only if he was left free to take the decision himself. But it had been taken by others.

"Poor Mrs. Tunney," she managed.

"I don't think Kathleen Tunney will be too upset, madam. She has a long-standing relationship with a divorced baker in Welstead. They'll get married, I imagine, as soon as the fuss has died down."

"He was popular, though, in the village."

Burchett considered. "He's been quite active in village

196

affairs, in fact Mrs. Hammond and I have found him obstructive. Most of the older generation suspect that he treated his niece very badly all those years ago, and they'll read between the lines of what happened this morning. It's not the sort of thing they talk about, even among themselves, except by way of hints and insinuations. There won't be any hostility to you, if that's what you're afraid of, thanks to your very tactful handling of this whole affair."

Celia suppressed a shudder at the word "tactful" and got rid of him as soon as she decently could. Her first concern was to get Bill released. At police headquarters in Welstead, she decided it would be unkind to brandish George Tunney's confession triumphantly under the nose of Detective-Inspector Ferris, and asked to speak to the head of the CID.

"Ah yes," he said when he had studied it. "This is the man who threw himself under a train early this morning at Welstead station. Very messy. Why? He didn't intend to kill Berridge, he'd only have got a year or two for losing his head and dumping him in the river, so why did he do it?"

"I've no idea," Celia murmured.

"Isn't someone else under arrest in connection with this case?"

"My head gardener at the nursery. I need him back on the job, everything's getting behind. He's in a cell downstairs."

"We'll get him out of there quick. I'll get the paperwork done now." He buzzed for his secretary to give instructions. "And tell Inspector Ferris I want to see him."

When Celia left five minutes later, armed with the document which would secure Bill's release, Ferris was waiting outside the door.

"What are you doing here, Mrs. Grant?" he demanded.

"Minding my own business."

"If you've gone to my superiors over my head, it is my business."

"Your business in there is to be ticked off for arresting

the wrong person and I hope he reduces you to the rank of constable.''

Bill was over the moon with excitement and gratitude.

"Oh Celia, you're a marvel, I never thought you'd bring it off, but you always do, don't you? I'll work overtime for weeks to make up for while I was in that filthy hole, and you can have as many insects in them glasshouses as you like, I'll never grouch about them again.''

She let him run on in this vein till they were halfway back to Melbury, then interrupted. "Now listen, Bill. None of this would have happened to you if you'd kept your head instead of beating Simon Berridge up that night in the Red Lion. It's time you settled down and found yourself a nice steady girl and started producing a row of little Wilkinses, because if you get into a mess like this again, I shan't lift a finger to get you out of it.''

He was surprised by her vehemence. He did not know that she was feeling very guilty, blaming herself for keeping quiet while two very dislikeable people hounded another human being to his death.

ABOUT THE AUTHOR

John Sherwood is a well-known British mystery author whose books include *A Shot in the Arm*, *A Botanist at Bay*, *Green Trigger Finger*, *Flowers of Evil*, *The Mantrap Garden*, and *Menacing Groves*. He and his wife live in Kent, in the south of England. A retired BBC executive, he enjoys gardening as a hobby.